Understanding the *Iliad*

By

Leon Golden

authorHOUSE™

1663 Liberty Drive, Suite 200
Bloomington, Indiana 47403
(800) 839-8640
www.AuthorHouse.com

© 2005 Leon Golden. All Rights Reserved.

No part of this book may be reproduced, stored in a retrieval system, or transmitted by any means without the written permission of the author.

First published by AuthorHouse 06/17/05

ISBN: 1-4208-1351-X (sc)
ISBN: 1-4208-1350-1 (dj)

Library of Congress Control Number: 2005903299

Printed in the United States of America
Bloomington, Indiana

This book is printed on acid-free paper.

Table of Contents

Preface vii

Introduction The Achievement of the *Iliad* ix

Chapter 1 The Gods, War, and the Human Condition 1

Chapter 2 Achilles 38

Chapter 3 The Relationship of the *Iliad* to Greek Tragic Theory and Practice 126

Notes 151

Index 155

Preface

Although the origins of Homer's *Iliad* reach back more than three thousand years, I take the view that this first—and perhaps greatest—work of literature in Western civilization should be read and studied as a contemporary document. By that I mean that I believe the subject of the *Iliad* to be no more or less than the human condition and that once we master the accidents of style and idiom of the poem, we achieve impressively profound insights into issues that are immediately relevant to ourselves. If the experiences of pathos, tragedy, heroism, endurance, suffering, and the struggle for enlightenment concerning the goals and values of human life are themes of great importance for us, then few works have more to offer than the *Iliad*.

In the course of reading this book, the reader will discover that I present some interpretations of the text that may not be in agreement with orthodox criticism of the poem. In every case, however, I have tried to make the *Iliad,* itself, offer support to my views by quoting, as fully as necessary, the passages in the poem that are the basis for my judgments. And while I have kept footnotes, in number and length, to a minimum, I have made ample use of the work of other scholars who have offered insightful contributions to our understanding of the *Iliad's* principal themes.

The *Iliad* is a rich and complex work, and much of the enjoyment I have found in teaching it over a period of some four decades is the discovery over time of deeper and deeper layers of significance within the poem. It is my hope that other readers will also share in this experience and in the great pleasure of *learning and inference (manthanein kai syllogizesthai)* which Aristotle recognized in the *Poetics* as the essential gift offered to mankind from encounters with great works of art.

I want to express my gratitude to my friends Scott Goins, Kevin Herbert, and Hans Mueller who have contributed much time and care to the reading of versions of my manuscript and made a number of valuable corrections and suggestions. They, of course, should not be held responsible for any of my comments and interpretations.

I wish to thank the editors and publishers of *Mnemosyne* for permission to use material in this book from my article published in that journal entitled, "Dios Apate and the Unity of Iliad 14" XLII (1989) 1-11. I also wish to thank the University Press of Florida for permission to reprint passages from L. Golden and O.B. Hardison, Jr., *Aristotle's Poetics: A Translation and Commentary for Students of Literature* (University Press of Florida, Gainesville, FL., 1981).

Tallahassee, Florida
October 2004
lgolden352@msn.com

Introduction

The Achievement of the *Iliad:*

An Overview

"Of all bookes extant in all kinds, Homer is the first and best." So begins the preface to Chapman's famed translation of the *Iliad* which was published as a complete text in 1611. It would not be difficult to find many today who agree with that judgment, at least as far as literature is concerned. My goal in this study is to contribute to the understanding of the enduring power that resides in this great epic that has attracted, entertained, and, most importantly, provided penetrating illumination about the human condition for many different kinds of audiences for nearly three millennia. The *Iliad* stands at the beginning of the literary tradition of our civilization, but we know that a long history of oral poetry preceded the fashioning of the form and content of the epic as we know it today. Our best judgment is that a master poet, of whom we know with certainty only his name, Homer, and his probable date, the eighth century B.C.E., took control of the large body of accumulated material concerned with various aspects of the Trojan War and, in a work of impressive artistic genius, creatively shaped and edited that material into a unified narrative covering fifty-one days of the ninth year of that war. The work itself reflects the interweaving of significant multiple themes, three of which, interconnected with each other, have special importance and prominence: (1) *the role of the gods in the narrative and thematic structure of the poem;* (2) *war, death, and the orthodox heroic code guiding behavior in war;* and (3) *the intellectual, emotional, and spiritual evolution of Achilles in the poem.*

A. The Function of the Gods in the *Iliad*

There are three important roles which the gods play in the poem. Willcock has described two of them as follows:[1]

> The participation of the gods in human activity may be thought of as taking place over a range of meaning between two extremes. At one end is the use of the god's name in a purely allegorical way, or even as a mere figure of speech. When Hephaistos is used for fire, or Ares for war...there is no religious implication, nor is the individuality of a particular god under consideration; one is simply using the name of the god for the power or function ascribed to him....At the other end of the scale are the occasions when the god acts as a totally independent agent in the human sphere, anthropomorphic, just like a human being and with human motives...At this end of the scale, the gods are little more than an aid to the plot; they are the divine machinery; their activity has as its aim the fulfillment of the Iliad story; there is little religious feeling about them.

The vast majority of references to the gods in the poem fall under the two categories which Willcock discusses, and as symbols of fire, war, passion, or intelligence, their principal function is to enrich the poetic diction of the poem. When the gods appear as aids to the development of the plot with the goal of fulfilling the Iliad story, they have an exclusively narrative function in moving the poem's action in the direction and toward the goal Homer has designed. In these two functions, the divine machinery of the poem does not make any significant *thematic* contribution to our understanding of the meaning of the *Iliad*. Not mentioned by Willcock, however, a very important third function of the gods in the poem, one that I would call "theological," where their words and actions define the conditions of human existence in the universe that is under their governance. I offer as an important

x

example of this "theological" function the following passage which will appear in our discussion later as well. Here at the beginning of book 4, Zeus admonishes Hera in a debate about the fate of Troy:

> "Do as you wish. Let not this quarrel become
> Hereafter a source of great strife between the two
> of us. But another thing I will tell you and you take it
> to heart. Whenever I am eager to destroy utterly a
> city And I choose one where there are men dear to
> you, Don't thwart my anger but let me do it.
> For willingly I grant this to you although my spirit is
> unwilling. For of the cities of men on earth that lie
> beneath the sun and the starry heavens, of these,
> sacred Troy was always most honored in my heart,
> And Priam and the people of ashen-spear Priam."
> The ox-eyed, queenly Hera answered him: "Three
> cities are by far most dear to me: Argos, Sparta,
> and Mycenae with its broad streets. These destroy
> utterly whenever they are hated in your heart.
> These I will not defend nor begrudge their fate."
> (4.37-54)

Statements such as this, expressing divine indifference to the fate of mortals, appear several times in the poem, and are of very great thematic importance to our understanding of the *Iliad*. These comments generally reflect a consistent point of view in which the lives of human beings, even those enjoying special favor among the gods or with intimate connections to them, are stripped of significance and not allowed to trouble the harmony or selfish interests of the divine powers who rule the universe. Zeus defines the status of mankind authoritatively when he laments the fate of the horses of Achilles as they mourn the dead Patroclus:

> "Ah, miserable pair, why did we give you to Lord
> Peleus a mortal, while you are deathless and
> ageless? Was it so that you could feel pain among
> luckless mortals? For nothing is more miserable
> than man Of all that breathes and crawls upon the
> earth." (17.443-47)

In these and similar passages, the gods appear in anthropomorphic form but their impact is not merely as the narrative agents Willcock has described; rather, they have a profound impact on the *meaning* of the *Iliad* for, in my view, these divine assessments of human insignificance, weakness, and vulnerability symbolize humanity's own cold, hard, and realistic vision of the place it occupies in the Homeric universe. Thus, I would suggest that the indifferent, at times contemptuous, attitude the gods express toward mankind in anthropomorphic terms should be interpreted as symbolic of the innate human susceptibility to dominance by the irrational, uncontrollable, and unpredictable forces at work in the world that create the pathos of the human condition. One impressive aspect of the heroism Homer celebrates in the *Iliad* is that the major characters of his poem are not subdued by the recognition of this pathos but, on their own, assume the burden of instilling meaning and value in mortal existence. The *Iliad* is a work that explores the way in which human beings, severed from the belief that external forces, supernatural or otherwise, exist in any way as their supportive allies, still respond courageously and effectively to their sobering destiny.

Mortals may and do pray and sacrifice to the gods, but without any assurance that their efforts will meet success, and they must always expect that the gods who may have protected them in the past will disappear from their presence at a critical moment in the future. The principal method that the heroes of the *Iliad* use to fill the moral vacuum of their universe is to make themselves agents of what we may call the *orthodox heroic code* on the battlefields of war. This code provides for the winning of enduring glory by exhibiting valor in killing or being killed in combat. Earning fame that will outlive mortal existence becomes the strategy for combating the emptiness, the pathos of dwelling in a universe in which human beings are otherwise all too vulnerable to external forces they cannot control. The orthodox heroes of the Trojan War deem glory that will live forever the proper antidote, the far preferable alternative to lives that will, otherwise, forever be without any significance. Thus, the kind of gods Homer depicts in his epic and the kind of lives many human beings choose to pursue are closely linked.

There is another important factor that we must keep in mind when interpreting the role of the gods in the action of the poem. This is the widely recognized concept known as "double motivation" or "over-determination" in offering probable or necessary causes for the actions that take place in the *Iliad*. Nearly always, and certainly for the most significant events in the poem, Homer supplies a psychologically persuasive reason, in human terms, for actions to occur even when he also, at the same time, ascribes those actions to divine will or intervention. Mark Edwards describes this process as follows:[2]

> Characteristically Homeric is the notion of "double motivation," by which many decisions and events are given one motivation on the divine level and one on the human. Often this is explicit: Ajax says that Achilles has "placed a savage temper in his breast" and goes on in the same breath to say that the *gods* put it there (9.629, 636); Similarly Diomedes says Achilles will return to the battle "when his inclination [*thumos*] and the god drive him." (9.703) Odysseus's poor oarsman, Elpenor, attributes his fatal fall from the roof to "the evil fate of the gods and too much wine." (*Odyssey* 11.61)
>
> A dramatic example is Achilles' great cry to terrify the Trojans away from Patroclus' body, magnified by Athena (18.217-18); it has been compared to the relief from the temple of Zeus at Olympia, which shows Heracles straining to support the burden of the sky while behind him Athena effortlessly lends a hand to make the feat possible. The dying Patroclus says to Hector, "Deadly destiny (*moira*) and Leto's son [Apollo] have killed me, and of men it was Euphorbus; you are the third to slay me" (16.849-50). Zeus drives on Hector "though Hector himself was in a fury" (15.604). This "over-determination," as it has been called, allows the poet to retain the interest of human characterization and action while superimposing upon it, for added dignity, the concern of the divinities.

Because one of Homer's greatest achievements, one that makes it possible for audiences of very different times and places to read his work as a highly relevant document for themselves, is his penetrating insight into the motivations driving human behavior, I will place especially great stress in this study on the psychologically realistic forces that unfold on the human plane to control the action of the *Iliad*.

To summarize: the functions of the gods in the *Iliad* can be viewed from three specific perspectives: (1) as symbols of aspects of human experience such as the goddess of wisdom, Athena, who in book 1 represents intelligent thought to Achilles as he ponders the possible slaughter of Agamemnon and as the goddess of love, Aphrodite, who in book 3 symbolizes the force of passionate desire to Helen; (2) as narrative elements available to the poet to move his plot in the direction he wanted it to go, and (3) as an expression of Homeric theology defining through the behavior and attitude of divine powers toward mankind the essential nature and limitations of the human condition as envisaged by the poet and experienced by the various characters he has created to inhabit the world of the *Iliad*. Also, throughout our reading of the poem we should be aware of the principle of "double motivation" which provides for *both* divine *and* human causation for the same events.

B. War, Death, and the Heroic Code

War is a major theme of the poem and provides the framework for those heroic code values that offer an affirmative response to the pathos threatening the human condition that is created by hostile external forces that are beyond mortal control. Schein offers us a useful statement of the traditional view of the role played by the heroic code of war in the epic:[3]

> Those who win such tangible honors also receive
> honor conceived abstractly; from this comes their
> *kleos*, "glory and reputation," what is said about
> them near and far, even when they are dead. To
> be sure, in the course of the *Iliad* Achilles comes to
> question and contradict the validity of the normative
> social value system. This disillusionment enhances
> Achilles' tragedy and constitutes part of Homer's
> critical exploration of the nature and conditions
> of heroism and of human life. *Nevertheless, for
> Achilles and for everyone else in the poem, there*

*is no real alternative. Life is lived and death is
died according to this code of values: to be fully
human—that is, to be a hero—means to kill or be
killed for honor and glory* (italics mine).

There is a great measure of truth to this account of the heroic
mentality, but it does not do full justice to the nuances of Homer's
vision of heroism. A more precise description of orthodox heroism,
because it emphasizes the spirit behind the inflicting and suffering
of death, rather than focusing on the acts themselves, is the
following statement by Owen:[4]

The hero is very far from being the master of his
fate, but one thing there is that is his—the power
to make his life glorious. Because it is all that a
man has and is, because it is brief and uncertain
and death ends all, man has the opportunity
to transform his life into a splendid thing by his
courage in risking it. Thus man himself imposes
a value on life, and he creates it out of the very
thing that robs it of its value. He cheats death of its
victory by making it the servant of his glory.

Owen's emphasis is on the willingness of the hero to take the
most valuable of his possessions, his tenuous mortal existence,
*and summon up the courage to risk it for enduing glory on the
battlefield.* In so doing, the heroic code warrior invests his life, a
possession of incalculable value because it is irreplaceable, with a
splendor that no circumstance of war or whim of fate can diminish.
I would, therefore, shift the emphasis in Schein's definition of
what it means to be a hero in the Homeric context from "to kill or
be killed for honor and glory" to the *demonstration of supreme
courage in submitting to the ultimate risk possible for a human
being in pursuit of honor and glory.*

There is one view of the heroic code in the *Iliad* which has
received rather wide attention but which appears to me to strike
a completely false note and which I will challenge in the next
chapter. This is a view but forward by J-P. Vernant, that has the
force of negating Owen's persuasive concept, cited above, which
recognizes that heroic behavior stamps life with meaning by
demonstrating the courage to *risk* life for a value more important

xv

than life itself. Vernant instead suggests that the heroic victory of the young warrior occurs when he *achieves* death in battle at the height of his powers and at the peak of his manhood, in full flower of youth, before old age and illness can corrupt and degrade his physical strength. I do not think that there is any evidence in the *Iliad*, or anywhere else, that supports the idea that soldiers have ever gone to war *aspiring* to die young and thus defeat the painful debilitation caused by old age and death.

C. Achilles

The third major theme of the *Iliad*, and in my view, the most important one, is that which focuses on Achilles. I have noted that the demonstration of valor in acts of killing and being killed is the route to heroic achievement for the orthodox heroes in the poem, but it is, significantly, *not* the mandate guiding the behavior of the most important of the characters in the epic, Achilles, to his climactic heroic destiny. We see this when we recall his rejection of the urgent pleading of Odysseus, one of Agamemnon's ambassadors seeking reconciliation between the two leaders in book 9, that he reenter the war since he could now easily win the greatest of heroic code prizes of glory, the slaying of Hector. Achilles greets this suggestion that embodies orthodox heroic code aspirations with contempt because his overwhelming motivation is vengeance, not glory, and by allowing the Trojan prince to remain alive and a lethal force against the Achaian army, he creates a potent instrument that serves his strategy for revenge. We should also remember that Achilles absents himself completely from war from book 1 until after the news of Patroclus's death is brought to him in book 18, which is a strong indication of his primary commitment to wreak vengeance on Agamemnon and the Achaian army; he even threatens at one time to leave the battlefield completely and return home—a move that is not at all in accord with the requirement of the orthodox heroic code for winning glory.

In the concluding phase of the *Iliad*, Achilles does reenter the war, but again to satisfy an even more furious appetite for revenge against the killer of Patroclus than the one he exhibited against Agamemnon and the Achaian army. The battlefield massacre of books 20-22 and the cruel desecration of Hector's corpse certainly fall within the killing and being killed theme of the heroic code, but their brutality shows that their origin lies in those darker levels of Achilles's psyche, where rage and vengeance fester, and do not represent the archetypal yearning for enduring glory. It is very clear that Achilles does not behave in accordance with the precepts of the orthodox heroic code warrior. His uniqueness surfaces in an even more eloquent way when, after the sustained torment of his enemy's dead body, there is a dramatic turnabout in his behavior. He demonstrates impressive compassion in his humane consolation of the grieving Priam, who comes as a suppliant to ransom his son, and in the generosity and kindness of his treatment of the body of the slain Hector in book 24.

It is my view that the role of Achilles as epic hero, and the special case of the heroic code he ultimately adopts, cannot be defined until the events of books 23 and 24 of the poem have unfolded and been carefully weighed. These two climactic books display an Achilles to us who is no longer, as before, driven by a vengeance-fed wrath toward friend and foe alike, nor one who still roams the battlefield as a berserk, insatiate killer.[5] The highest rung of heroism that Achilles attains is not, in the view I will present, the mad orgy of lives taken and bodies desecrated in rage, but the magnificent act of self-mastery that unfolds in book 24; here in Walter Burkert's sympathetic account, he is the source of an unparalleled amount of compassion in the *Iliad* as he erects a bridge of empathy in creating an "I/Thou" relationship with Priam, the body of whose son he had earlier brutally mutilated,[6] and which he now treats with the loving care and respect of a father or older brother. Homer does not allow any other warrior in the poem to approach Achilles either in the savagery of his zeal for vengeance or the sublimity of his compassion for human suffering.

There are important reasons why we must consider the story of Achilles, in the shape it takes as a depiction of his evolving character, to be the essential story of the *Iliad*. He, alone, of all the major characters is present, and present in impressively different ways, as a controlling force, in both the first and last book of the epic; moreover, his powerful influence is felt throughout the intervening books as a determining force not paralleled by any other character. His actions are, thus, the one dominant, unifying theme linking the beginning, middle, and end of the *Iliad*. Also, and most importantly, although he comes to know, equally with the enemies he has defeated, Hector and Priam, the wounding pathos of the human condition in the Homeric universe, he discovers, ultimately and after much pain, the means within himself to transmute his response to that pathos into a better and finer expression of the human spirit. Of immense importance is the fact that Achilles, uniquely among all the heroes in the poem, undergoes change, evolution, and maturation during the course of the traumatic suffering that occurs to him over the fifty-one days in which the poem unfolds. In the history of literature, a story which focuses on the evolving development of a central character toward greater maturity, wisdom, and insight has come to be known as a *Bildungsroman*, a category to which I believe the *Iliad*, in essence, is closely related and so I will view Achilles from the perspective of a hero of such a work who must struggle with explosions of vengeful rage that destructively escalate from book 1 through the beginning of book 23 without liberating him from the pain and suffering he endures; but who finally experiences a revelation in the final two books of the poem that leads him to embrace a world view far different and more profound than the one with which he began the poem.

I will devote my third chapter to a detailed interpretation of Achilles's role in the poem. But I note here that there have been a number of clashing views about Achilles that differ from the one I will emphasize, and we are indebted to Mark Edwards for helpfully describing the range of these discordant interpretations for us; his discussion of the problem will merit further consideration later.[7]

In reading the *Iliad,* we should be guided by its character as a riveting and insightful *contemporary* study of important themes relating to the human condition. I designate it as *contemporary* because of its *universality,* which cannot be defeated by the passage of time and changes of custom and taste. There are those, however, in the past and present, who view the *Iliad* (and other ancient texts) from a very different perspective, one in which these works are restricted in their significance to the specific societies and historical epochs in which they first appeared, and thus must be understood primarily as documents bearing historical witness to those societies and epochs. Readers interested in guidance on the most rewarding approach to be taken in reading the *Iliad* and many other ancient texts will find instructive a debate that took place on this issue in the early decades of the twentieth century between the great German scholar Ulrich von Wilamowitz-Moellendorff and the distinguished American classicist, Harold Cherniss.[8] Using Thucydides as an example, Cherniss noted that there are practitioners of three disciplines who have a valid interest in his work: (1) the historian who uses it as source material for reconstructing actual historical events; (2) the historiographer who is interested in the historian's methodology; and (3) students of literature who will view it as a dramatic prose narrative. Cherniss acknowledges that all three of these activities are important, but that they must not be confused with each other and, above all, that the literary study of Thucydides or any other prose or poetic text with literary aspirations must not be subordinated to the purposes of the historian. He points out that although literary texts can legitimately be used as ancillary materials by historians, that in no way deprives them of independent, autonomous existence as the products of the human imagination, any more than mathematics, because it is used as an ancillary methodology in the natural sciences, loses in any way its autonomous existence as a completely separate and co-equal discipline.

The approach which contradicts this principle is the one pursued by Wilamowitz, who argued that to understand any poet— and here he uses Aristophanes as an example—"the events and personalities of Athenian history must have been so thoroughly studied that one can enter into the transitory mood of each year and so that the forms of public life, which were immediate data for the poet and audience, remain ever present for us too without special reminder" (282). Under these arguments, literature loses its autonomous position as a universal manifestation of the human spirit and becomes an instrument for communicating particular facts relevant to a particular time and place in history. Cherniss points out that Wilamowitz's approach to the study of literature requires that the critic engage in "the reconstruction of the environment" in which the work was produced and also to transform himself "into a contemporary of the author" (283). In opposition to this position, Cherniss argues persuasively (284-85):

> Even a Wilamowitz with all his knowledge of vase painting, Greek institutions, and Athenian history, cannot think and feel as did a contemporary of Aristophanes and could not do so were the monuments for study at his disposal a thousand times as many as they are. *Knowing* that Dionysus was a god to those who still delighted in his ridiculous antics upon the stage, and *feeling* that

he is a god even while enjoying him as a clown
– between these two states is a gulf that no
erudition can bridge, a gulf not due to time and
the absence of material evidence....In the case of
ancient literature there is not adequate material to
enable the student to gain even a fairly complete
theoretical knowledge of the environment in which
were produced most of the works with which he is
concerned; to believe that one can know the events
and personages of Athenian history so intimately
as to be able to detect the transitory mood of
each year is to deceive oneself by taking for
objective truth the tenuous phantoms of historical
reconstructions.

Cherniss points out that Wilamowitz's approach to literary
study makes the poem or play into "a single state in a hypothetical
development in which the author is only an accident or at most
an agent of forces which transcend him and of which he is
unconscious" (285). He rejects such a view of literary study as
inadequate and uses the strong words of E.R. Curtius to assert the
reasons for his rejection. He quotes Curtius as viewing his rejected
view (286) as consisting in this:

to speak not of the object but of the causes, not
of the essence but of the relationships; not to
interpret the works, but to investigate the material,
the environment, the influences; a method which
ever remains in the sphere of the preliminary,
the irrelevant, the extrinsic, and reduces true
scholarship to erudition in what is not worth
knowing.

Cherniss concludes his critique of Wilamowitz's approach
with a claim for the universality of the literary work, as opposed
to the narrowly restricted role that it would play if it were only a
historical artifact, of interest primarily to the historian who desires
to reconstruct a past epoch, and having no relevance to those
living at other times and places. Cherniss judges that "only a
madman would even wish to transmute himself into a member of
that audience in order to appreciate what could have no meaning

for men at any other time or place" (289). What makes a literary work of art significant, Cherniss argues, is that it is an autonomous entity existing "independently of its author and of the accidental circumstances of its production" (290). The independent existence of the work of art alone bestows universality on it and makes possible the direct approach to a work of art by an audience and makes this direct approach "the only possible way of comprehension and appreciation" (290). Cherniss defines the universality of the work of art as the significance it has "for all men as men at all times and places" (290) which it derives from the common store of ideas, emotions, and values that are the essential possession of culture. In reasserting the autonomous existence and significance of literary works of art, Cherniss denies that they are the "automatic by-product of external forces" and asserts that their value as source material for the historian is inferior to their value "for men as human beings." He makes that point decisively in the last paragraph of his article:

> We pride ourselves mightily on our "true historical sense," of which, says one famous modern classicist [Wilamowitz], "Lessing and Gibbon had scarcely a notion, for they thought that man in all ages is essentially the same." Perhaps that is why the writings of Lessing and Gibbon can still be read with understanding today while the books of the new scholarship are antiquated after a decade. When the Hellenist no longer believes in man as *man*, he may as well shut his books, for he has confessed that he can never understand them. (291)

The quality of universality in great ancient texts, recognized by Cherniss, is brought into direct contact with Homer by Joachim Latacz.[9] Of Homer's timelessness, Latacz writes:

> Homer's influence, right from the start, had rested on his very freedom from direct time conditioning, that is, on time-independent qualities. The history of Homer reception among the Greeks themselves, the Romans, and modern readers is proof of

> Homer's obvious quality for all times, especially when an attempt was made to deny it.

Latacz reinforces this affirmation of Homeric universality with an emphatic recognition of the proximity of Homer to the modern world:[10]

> In recent years, much time has been spent, especially in Germany, explaining how distant Homer is from us. The talk was of the "alterity" or the "otherness" of Homer, of his "nonrelevance," of the (for us) "last extremity of incomprehensible foreignness" of Homeric society....Behind such expressions lies above all an overestimation of our inherent uniqueness, which strikes one as absurd against the background of the six hundred thousand years of human history. The period that divides us from Homer amounts to not much more than eighty generations. The foreignness between Homer and ourselves, apparent chiefly in external forms, shrinks away in the face of the obvious constants taken together. Each reader will discover for herself or himself what is immutable in human thoughts, values, and aspirations...

I suggest that we can gain control of the universality of the *Iliad*, of the high degree of its relevance to ourselves, by reading the poem, as I propose to do in this study, as a *Bildungsroman*. That is, as an insightful record of the evolution and maturation of Achilles in the context of his poignant struggle against the pathos of the human condition, which for him means against humiliation, loss, grief, and, most of all, against his own flawed and destructive responses of rage and revenge to the intimidating forces that confront him. In the end, however, we will see, as one perceptive critic has said, "the central hero of the poem, Achilles, move toward disillusionment and death to reach a new clarity about human existence"[11] and with that clarity will come initiation into the heroic code of the human spirit with rewards, transcendent and triumphal, that are far more significant than the enduring fame of victory on the battlefield. In this way, we will come to see how Homer has successfully designed his great epic, in Latacz's words, "to reflect the world in all its characteristics in a work of verbal art and to explain it meaningfully."

Chapter 1

The Gods, War, and the Human Condition

In this chapter, I want to focus on Homer's characterization of the human condition in the *Iliad*. It is a major thrust of my interpretation that Homer uses the divine framework of his poem to describe—sometimes subtly and sometimes much more emphatically—the nature and boundaries of mortal existence. Homer attributes to the anthropomorphic gods of the epic consistent attitudes toward humanity, and whenever those attitudes are manifest, the gods play what I call a "theological" role in the poem; that is, comments by the gods about human beings and their interaction with them become direct evidence the poet wants us to have about the true significance, the reality of what it means to be human in the world of the epic. I want to review now the most important passages which bear on divine evaluations of the human condition. In my introductory chapter, I gave two examples of the theological dimension I attribute to the gods in the poem. One of these related to the cool indifference with which Zeus and Hera were willing to allow their favorite cities and worshipers to be destroyed as a favor to each other, and the other to Zeus's contemptuous view of human beings as the most miserable of all creatures who inhabit the earth. Sometimes divine pronouncements about human beings are deadly serious in their indifference, hostility, or contempt; sometimes the negative emotions are real but presented with whimsical or even comic overtones. In book 1, Achilles begs Thetis to intercede with Zeus to punish Agamemnon and the Achaians for the insult he has

Leon Golden

received from having been stripped of his prize. Thetis is most willing to do this but remarks that

> Zeus went to Ocean, Yesterday for a feast with the Ethiopians. All the gods followed along. On the twelfth day from now he will return to Olympus, And I shall go then to Zeus' house with its bronze threshold and I will supplicate him and I think I will persuade him. (1.423-27)

This charming story of gods on a holiday makes no major contribution to the narrative direction of the *Iliad*, but it is of definite thematic significance. The depiction of unapproachable gods on vacation at a time when humans need them lays the foundation for the motif of divine indifference to the human condition that is one central aspect of the relationship of the gods to mankind throughout the poem. To this profile of gods who sever themselves from human contact for a period of entertainment and relaxation should be added the depiction of their easy proneness to violence among themselves at the end of book 1, which erases any suspicion of moral superiority on the divine level. When Thetis makes her appeal on behalf of Achilles to Zeus, Hera is watching and confronts Zeus with her suspicion that he has agreed to help Achilles in obtaining the vengeance he wants against Agamemnon and the Achaian army which acquiesced in inflicting dishonor on him. Zeus responds with the threat of physical violence against Hera, and Hephaestus intervenes with an account of the injury he suffered at the hands of Zeus when he previously came to the defense of his mother. Some critics and readers have taken this scene as lighthearted and amusing, but I think that this is a serious mistake in the light of the consistent depiction Homer gives us of the divine/human relationship. In this context, Willcock offers a better analysis:[1]

> We may notice the artistic effect of the ending of the book. There has been disease, death, and bitter quarreling among the men down below; and for a moment, it looked as if the dispute might disturb the easy tenor of life among the gods. But they soon realize that it is not worth troubling themselves "for

Understanding the Iliad

the sake of mortals" (574); and after a pleasant evening they go quietly home to bed.

The lack of essential importance of humanity in the eyes of the gods is a theme that we will see repeated in much grimmer circumstances as we proceed. Edwards connects divine indifference in this scene with the lack of any moral conscience on the part of the gods vis-á-vis human beings:[2]

> ...for the gods presented to us, though impressive for their deadly power, have shown no superior conception of justice, no concern for mankind apart from a demand for men's respect and an affection for their particular favorites, and no interests beyond their own honor and their wonderful parties.

Willcock is surely correct to call attention to divine contempt for the lives and destinies of mankind when the gods reject the idea that any human event can be important enough to interfere with their own luxurious existence; and Edwards is certainly right to emphasize the amorality of the gods' governance of the universe mankind inhabits, which has the consequence of placing the heavy burden of finding meaning and value in existence solely on human shoulders.

We have noted how, in the opening scene of book 4, the assembly of the gods, the theme of divine indifference to human beings deepens into divine contempt for mortals. With chilling disdain for humanity's value and importance, we recall the easy trade-off of great and populous cities, Troy, Argos, Sparta, and Mycenae made by Zeus and Hera to sate their lust for power and vengeance. Willcock, for one, correctly assesses the tone of this scene:[3]

> The speech that follows shows the utter ruthlessness and selfishness of the goddess; she will willingly allow Zeus to destroy her three favorite cities in Greece at anytime in the future, if he will support her wish to destroy Troy now.

I would only add to Willcock's comment that Zeus's ready acquiescence in this arrangement shows *his* "utter ruthlessness

Leon Golden

and selfishness" also. Jasper Griffin perceptively comments on the passage as follows:[4]

> This scene, which immediately precedes the outbreak of fighting in the *Iliad*, is a nightmare picture for men. Punctilious service of the gods, even divine affection, is no defense; the will of another god ('for I too am a god') overrules any human claim. "What has Troy done to you?" Zeus asks Hera, and she need not even answer. Justification is not the point, and the gods are not limited to a tragic attitude toward the sight of human suffering: they can always change their viewpoint and enjoy the spectacle. Finally, they can turn away their attention altogether.

Consistent with the tone of the scene we have just discussed is the passage from book 8, where Hera says to Athena:

> "Child of Aegis bearing Zeus no longer can I allow us to make war against Zeus For the sake of mortals. Let one perish And another live, however it turns out. And let him judge, pondering these things in his heart, for Trojans and Danaans, as is reasonable." (8.427-31)

Commenting on this passage, Kirk accurately notes, "the futility of gods suffering [on account of mortals] is a recurrent theme: men can die or not as they please."[5]

We find a most important insight into the theology of the *Iliad* in book 14, where an extremely troubling expression of divine indifference to the sufferings of mankind occurs. The events of this book merit special emphasis. First, we must note the tripartite structure of the book, a framework in which the famous central segment, the "deception of Zeus" scene, stands in shocking emotional contrast to the anguished conference of Greek leaders which precedes, and the savage scenes of war which follow it. It is important for us not to miss the important role the "deception of Zeus" scene plays as a major link in the network of theological statements concerning divine indifference to mankind, although some critics have been so distracted by the tone of this central

Understanding the Iliad

section of book 14 that they have missed the ominous connection between this scene and the other, grimmer components of book 14. Cedric Whitman, for example, writes: "The seduction of Zeus, developed at length for its own sake, is entirely in the spirit of comedy."[6] That comment misses the important point that the deeply disturbing nature of the "seduction of Zeus" scene arises precisely because the divine behavior it describes clashes so sharply with the human suffering which serves as the prologue and epilogue to it in book 14. We must realize that Homer creates an important thematic unity in the *Iliad* out of the contrast between the way the gods apply themselves spiritedly to anthropomorphic indulgences in power, pleasure, lust, and deception, and the sordid reality of human suffering which frames the central section of book 14. Karl Reinhardt perceptively warns us that we must not forget that amidst scenes depicting laughter and seduction amongst the gods of Homer lie stories of divine cunning, deception, shackling, insurrection, and secrecy, which emerge on occasion as darker characterizations of divine behavior.[7] Owen offers a useful account of the meaning and tone of the seduction scene:[8]

> The episode is excellently well placed to break the account of the long day's battle. Set in the midst of the endless fighting, there is in it the relief of beauty, of humour, a complete change of scene, character, tone. We are back in the light, frivolous atmosphere of Olympus. There seems also, in its sharp contrast with bitter scenes of human suffering, something of irony. This is the heavenly aspect of that desperate struggle on the plain below. Perhaps the poet did not intend this effect; and yet the words he gives to Achilles later on seem to show him aware of the contrast.... "For this is the lot the gods have spun for miserable mortals, that they should live in pain, while they themselves are without sorrow" (XXIV,525-26)

I would, however, add here that Owen is too cautious in appraising the stark Homeric distinction between the suffering humans must endure and existences immune from serious and lasting tribulations enjoyed by the gods. Owen's reference to

Leon Golden

Achilles's comparison of the lot of mortals and divinities is right on the mark and merits greater emphasis in his commentary.

In the first section of book 14, we find deep despair on the human level. The military situation has turned against the Achaian army, generals are wounded, and the army is in disarray. Agamemnon is ready to flee Troy, but Odysseus denounces his cowardly plan and Diomedes suggests that, though the wounded officers cannot go into battle, they can go down to the battlefield and marshal and encourage the troops who are in a physical condition to fight. This plan is adopted as part 1 of book 14 comes to an end. In the second, central section of the book, the seduction scene, we move from the human plane to the divine environment and, as Owen has seen, by changing the mood and tone so radically, Homer demonstrates to us the vast differences that exist between human and divine lives. On Olympus, the events of war that so painfully oppress suffering human beings are transformed into a game, an amusement in which Hera undertakes to outwit Zeus so that the aid he promised Thetis he would give to the Trojans in support of Achilles's wrath at Agamemnon might be nullified. Her strategy, aimed at one of Zeus's most vulnerable characteristics, his sexual appetite, is a process of seduction carried out like a military campaign. We begin with an account of Hera dressing for her encounter with Zeus:

> First she cleansed every stain from her lovely skin
> With ambrosia, then anointed herself richly with
> oil, Ambrosial, pleasing, and fragrant. If this were
> just shaken in the house of Zeus with its threshold
> of Bronze, the scent nevertheless would travel
> to heaven and earth. With this she anointed her
> beautiful body and having combed her Hair, with
> her hands she braided her locks, bright, beautiful,
> And ambrosial flowing from her immortal head.
> Then she put around herself an ambrosial robe that
> Athena had delicately worked for her with skill and
> placed many Embroideries on it and she pinned it
> on her breast with brooches of gold. And she girded
> herself with a belt fitted with a hundred tassels
> and she placed In her pierced ears earrings with
> three mulberry drops. And great was the grace that
> flashed forth from them. And with a veil beautiful

Understanding the Iliad

and new she, bright among the Goddesses,
covered herself from above; and it was as White
as the sun. And beneath her bright feet She bound
beautiful sandals. (14.170-86)

In one sense, this is an "arming" scene that parallels the type-scene of a warrior arming for combat that Homer uses several times in the *Iliad*.[9] We might compare it to the following description of the arming of Paris before his encounter with Menelaus:

And god-like Alexandros, the husband of fair-haired
Helen, put around his shoulders the beautiful armor.
First he placed On his legs beautiful greaves fitted
with silver clasps; Then he Donned about his chest
the breastplate of his brother, Lycaon, and It fitted
him well. And about his shoulders he cast a silver-studded Sword made of bronze and then a shield
large and sturdy. And on His mighty head he placed
a well-wrought helmet with horse-hair plume. And
fearfully did the crest nod from above. (3.328-37)

Paris is going to escape the lethal consequences of hand-to-hand combat in this scene by fleeing the battlefield when his life is threatened while other soldiers, arming themselves the way he does, will be caught up in the inevitable process of killing and being killed. Hera's arming scene can be considered a parody and mockery of human warriors preparing for battle for they face death while the consequence for Hera, after her initial success, is merely another angry confrontation with Zeus which she is able to deflect without damage to herself.

Having donned the "armor" that would prove most effective against Zeus, Hera develops a further offensive strategy against him that is designed to remove him, for some time, as a blocking force interfering with her intentions. She proceeds to deceive Aphrodite with a false story that will put into her hands a magical device that will give her the power to instill passion and love into anyone who crosses her path whom she wishes to control. With that accomplished, Hera secures the services, by bribery, of the minor deity, Sleep, to apply his numbing power to Zeus after the seduction takes place and so prolong the time that he will remain isolated from war. Hera's maneuvers work perfectly and Zeus

Leon Golden

falls victim to the contrived enhancements to her beauty and the irresistible power of Aphrodite's potent love charm. Homer describes the climactic moment of seduction as follows:

> Beneath them, the bright earth brought forth A bed
> of fresh grass, and dewy lotus, and crocus, And
> hyacinth, soft and thick, that kept them high off the
> ground. And both of them lay within it And were
> clothed in a beautiful, golden cloud And glistening
> drops of dew fell from it. (14.347-51)

After this, Sleep does his job well and Hera's will, for the time being, is accomplished. Clothed in a golden cloud, bathed by glistening dew, resting on a soft bed of fresh grass and thick, soft flowers, Zeus and Hera on Mt. Ida bring the central section of book 14 to a conclusion in a moment of impassioned ecstasy. Nowhere else in this poem where rage, violence, and slaughter are such dominant themes do we have so exultant an evocation of pure joy. Less than fifty lines later, however, as we return to the human plane of existence in the concluding phase of book 14, the situation for mortals clashes bitterly with the games which the gods play. First Ajax strikes Hector with a boulder that drops him to the ground where he "vomited up a cloud of black blood" (14.445). Later Peneleos kills Ilioneus:

> And Peneleos struck him beneath the brow at the
> base of the eye And thrust the eyeball out. His
> sword Went straight through the eye and the nape
> of the neck. And he sank down stretching out both
> of his hands. Peneleos drawing his sharp sword
> drove it into the center of his Neck and struck off his
> head along with the Helmet. And the great spear
> was still planted In the eye. Peneleos holding it up
> like the head of a poppy Showed it to the Trojans...
> (14.496-500)

Other brutal deaths follow to bring book 14 to a close, a book which graphically teaches us that the counterpart on the human level to the lustful sport with which the gods amuse themselves is brutal death in the grim and devastating massacres of war. A number of critics have emphasized the importance of this

Understanding the Iliad

wide difference between the character of divine and human existence as a theme that is essential to understanding the world view of the *Iliad*. Hölscher, describing the contrast between the easy life of the gods and the troubled lives of mortals, correctly states that war on the human plane is a form of entertainment for the gods.[10] Reinhardt accurately defines the nature of divine existence in the *Iliad* as lacking seriousness because in spite of all their angry arguments and threats and occasional physical violence—as Hephaestus has reminded us at the end of book 1—they are totally free from death, destruction, and the awful suffering that clouds the fates of mortals. He sees the battles in which the gods participate as mirroring human combat, except for the absence of one terrible ingredient: true danger.[11] Burkert notes that the opposition between the lighthearted lives of the gods and the deadly serious fate of human beings is essential for understanding the world of the *Iliad,* where divine insouciance is an impressive manifestation of total divine freedom and security.[12] Seidensticker persuasively explores the thematic connections between Homer's use of scenes of divine levity or divine combat unattended by any real danger and events involving deep human suffering. In this connection, he refers to the events which we have been discussing in book 14 where Hera's parodic "arming" for her encounter with Zeus and the frivolous seduction which ensues occur in the very midst of the murderous combat of mortals that unfolds by the ships; and he makes his point more emphatic by citing the actions of gods who risk nothing essential in their mutual combat in book 21, an event that Homer sets directly after Achilles's bloody acts of "butchery" at the River Skamander and before the death of Hector that occurs in the following book. Seidensticker correctly assesses the significance of these scenes of divine immunity to pain and suffering as forming a significant contrast to the inescapable tragedy of human existence, a tragedy that is deepened and made more painful through the superiority and lighthearted irresponsibility of the gods.[13]

So far, we have seen an ominous and consistent message for human beings in passages relating to the theological framework of the *Iliad*: it emerges from the picture of gods "on vacation" and prone to violence in book 1, from their conscienceless acquiescence in the destruction of their own favorite cities to please another god in book 4, and from the tripartite structure of book 14, in which divine dalliance on Mt. Ida disconcertingly

Leon Golden

interrupts the oppressive atmosphere of human suffering and slaughter on the battlefield below. The message is that humanity is on its own, fragile, vulnerable, and dependent only on itself for the possibility of surviving and prospering in the world it inhabits. The overwhelming indifference and/or disdain in which the gods hold mankind appears in three other passages in the poem. In book 16, Zeus ponders whether or not to intervene in the struggle between Sarpedon and Patroclus in order to save Sarpedon, and says to Hera:

> "Alas, Sarpedon, the dearest of men to me is fated
> to be subdued by Patroclus, the son of Menoetius.
> In two ways does the heart in my breast ponder
> whether still living I snatch him from tearful battle
> and place him in the Rich land of Lycia, or I let him
> die now at Patroclus' hands." And ox-eyed, Hera
> his lady, answered: "Most dread son of Cronus,
> what a thing you have said! A mortal man, long ago
> fated to his destiny Do you wish to free him again
> from hateful death? Do it. But not all the other gods
> will approve it. But I will tell you this and cast it into
> your heart. If you send Sarpedon living to his home
> consider that some other One of the gods will also
> wish hereafter to send his dear son out of harsh
> battle. For many sons of the immortals fight around
> Priam's great city. And on these you will send dread
> wrath." (16.433-49)

Zeus reluctantly bows to Hera's admonition while shedding tears of blood for his own son whose life he will not save because such an act would disturb the tenor of life for the gods on Olympus. In the theology of the *Iliad,* the gods care so little for human beings, even those who are dearest to them, that their expressions of minimal grief for them can only evoke pained outrage on the human level. Griffin, a most astute commentator on divine/human relationships in the poem, says the following in relation to Sarpedon's death:[14]

> Sarpedon is Zeus' own son, and he too must be
> allowed to meet his death at Patroclus' hands,
> though he is "dearest of men" to his father, who

Understanding the Iliad

looks on in pity but does not save. Sarpedon is indeed honoured with a supernatural sign of the grief of Zeus, a fall of bloody rain, and is given posthumous honours in Lycia; but this is such cold comfort that the hero's friend Glaucus cries bitterly: "The best of men is dead, Sarpedon, the son of Zeus; he does not even help his own child."

In the world of the *Iliad*, grief, pain, and suffering characterize mortal life but are foreign to the life of the gods, who can easily deflect them with the infinite resources for a hedonistic lifestyle available to them. Griffin remarks:[15]

All the actions of the gods are easy; so then is their whole life. They are "blessed gods" and "gods who live at ease". Their physical circumstances are those of delight; on Olympus, there "the blessed gods enjoy pleasure forever" (vi.46). There they feast and drink, and have to entertain them the music of Apollo and the Muses (i.603). To complete their bliss, they need only one thing more: a subject to interest them. They hate to look at Hades and the realm of the dead; the subject is provided by the existence of mortal men and their sufferings. The nature of men and gods is exactly calculated to set off and define that of each other. Thus, as the life of gods is blessed, so that of men is miserable; as they are typically so in a Homeric phrase for "men."

The next commentary on mortal insignificance, one that I have noted previously, comes at book 17.443-47, where Zeus pities the immortal horses of Achilles who are mourning for the slain Patroclus. Of these horses, Zeus says:

"Ah, miserable pair, why did we give you to Lord Peleus, A mortal, while you are deathless and ageless? Was it so that you could feel pain among luckless mortals? For nothing is more miserable than man of all that breathes and crawls upon the earth."

Leon Golden

On this passage, Griffin remarks that Zeus "is moved to pity by the unhappiness of Achilles's immortal horses, which are mourning for Patroclus. The horses belong to heaven, and their grief seems to move Zeus more than Patroclus's death."[16]

Finally, in a conversation with Poseidon in book 21, Apollo says:

> "Earthshaker, you would not speak of me as having sense If I should go to war with you for the sake of mortals, Pitiful creatures who like leaves sometimes Are full of vital fire, eating the fruit of the field And sometimes perish lifelessly. But very quickly let us cease from strife, and let men themselves struggle. (21.462-67)

This is one of the most emphatic assessments we have of how insignificant human beings are in the larger scheme of the universe from the divine perspective. There is one more general observation to be made, and Griffin, again, is our guide to it, that puts the seal of inconsequentiality, from the divine perspective, on mortal lives by recognizing the role of the gods as divine observers of the spectacle of human suffering.[17] This is the realization that the gods find the events of war, men involved in acts of killing and being killed, a diversion not unlike that which they would experience if they were attending a sporting competition or dramatic festival. Griffin notes ancient commentators were "shocked" by the apparent cruelty involved in the gods serving as an audience for human travail and tried hard, but unconvincingly, to find a justification for it.

What is communicated in the theology of the *Iliad* as I have described it is one of the most important thematic elements of the poem: the fragility and vulnerability of what it means to be human *sub specie aeternitatis*. It is my view that the profile of indifferent, contemptuous anthropomorphic gods I have presented symbolizes and characterizes the actual conditions which human beings in the *Iliad* recognize as the reality governing their world. If the gods can absent themselves at will from human contact; if to feed their vanity, lust, and egotistical impulses they can trade off their favorite cities to each other for destruction; if, rather than compassionately intervening, they can leave human beings to their own suffering and misery in order to avoid disturbing the hedonistic atmosphere

Understanding the Iliad

of Olympus; if they can engage in the sport of deceiving and seducing each other while sordid forms of death and physical desecration haunt the final moments of mortal heroes; if they can feel more anguish for the suffering of divine horses than for mortal men; if human lives mean no more to them than pitiful leaves which briefly live and then die; and if the spectacle of warriors killing and being killed is a form of entertainment for them, then the threat of ultimate absurdity hovers over humanity. That the *Iliad* is *not* a poem asserting the absurdity of human existence, but one that validates heroism on several levels is due to its humanistic fervor that explores the capacity of human beings, under duress, to mobilize their own resources heroically in order to fill with meaning and values of their own design and discovery the moral void that exists in the universe. Success in this endeavor is most commonly achieved in the poem through adherence to the value system we know as the "heroic code" of Homeric warfare. As we shall see, this warrior ethic is not, however, the last word Homer has to say about the process of creating value and significance in human existence, because the orthodox warrior code, although of wide application, does not describe the complex nature of the central figure of the poem, Achilles, and it is not the theme that is celebrated in the climactic final two books of the epic. I have referred earlier to Seth Schein's definition of the heroic code[18] which, in part, states that:

> for Achilles and for everyone else in the poem,
> there is no real alternative. Life is lived and death
> is died according to this code of values: to be fully
> human—that is, to be a hero—means to kill or be
> killed for honor and glory.

I will discuss more fully later why I believe the orthodox heroic code is not the *Iliad's* ultimate answer to mankind's quest for meaning in the *Iliad,* but since it plays such a prominent role in the poem and has been understood or misunderstood in a number of ways, it deserves our careful attention. The heroic code is—strictly speaking—a military set of values which confers honor and permanent remembrance on those who exhibit heroism in combat.

Three important passages in the *Iliad* define the essentials of this concept for us. First, there is Hector's conversation with his wife, Andromache, before returning to battle in book 6. She has

Leon Golden

pleaded with him to exert caution and protect himself from death and his family from the harm that his death will cause them and he replied:

> "My wife, all these things are a concern to me but
> I feel Terrible shame before the Trojans and their
> wives, With their trailing robes if like a coward I
> shunned war Nor does my spirit bid me since I
> have learned to be brave always and to fight in the
> front ranks of the Trojans earning great glory for my
> father and for myself." (6.441-46)

We observe here that the heroic code privileges public responsibilities that are capable of generating honor and glory over private relationships and obligations. We see this especially well when, in spite of Andromache's deep sorrow and fear, Hector offers this prayer for his infant son while his sorrowing mother stands by:

> "Zeus and all the other gods: grant that this son
> of mine become, just as I am, outstanding among
> Trojans, and as brave In his strength, and to rule
> Ilion with might. And one day someone might say
> that he is far better than his father when he returns
> from war. And may he bear bloody spoils, when he
> has killed his enemy. And may his mother rejoice."
> (6.476-81)

His wife's tears and his own child's terrified reaction to the fearful appearance of his father just back from the front lines of combat do nothing to lessen the heroic code's inescapable imperative to privilege glory won from killing and being killed over any other human emotion or aspiration. For the great heroic code warrior—and Hector is certainly one of the greatest of them—the winning of glory, of *kleos* that will live on in the words of the poet and the memory of mankind, is the one weapon he has for countering the atmosphere of divine disdain and indifference that threatens to make the human condition trivial and absurd. We have seen earlier that Owen recognized that "the hero has the opportunity to transform his life into a splendid thing by his courage in risking it. Thus man himself imposes a value on his

Understanding the Iliad

life and...cheats death of its victory by making it the servant of his glory."[19]

The relationship between the demands and rewards of the heroic code and the price that may have to be paid for those rewards is the theme of the conversation between Sarpedon and Glaucus in book 12. Sarpedon reminds Glaucus that on one level it is the considerable perquisites which they enjoy as members of the aristocratic class that imposes upon them the obligations as warriors and chieftains to risk their lives in battle. On a much deeper level, however, their commitment to the dangers of war is based on the inescapable fact of their personal mortality, which must either fade into bleak meaninglessness, or be elevated to enduring significance by the winning of glory. Sarpedon advises Glaucus:

> "Ah, my friend, if we, two, having escaped this war
> were always going to be immortal and ageless I
> myself would Never again fight among the foremost
> Nor send you into battle where men win glory. But
> now since death stands over us in countless forms
> which it is not possible For a mortal to escape or
> avoid, Let us go forth either to bestow glory on
> someone or to win glory from someone." (12.322-
> 28)

The heroic code provides a means for overcoming death without meaning by privileging death ennobled by glory, whether in the grasping of it or the yielding of it, in the arena of combat. Sarpedon's speech illustrates very well Owen's comment that the hero has the power to make his brief and uncertain life into something "splendid" by risking it in the pursuit of enduring fame, and that is especially true when we reflect on how alone and vulnerable human beings are in the universe administered by uncaring forces far beyond their control.

Perhaps the most famous statement of the heroic code comes in the lines spoken by Hector in book 22 as he faces imminent death at the hands of Achilles:

> "Now evil death is close at hand and not far away,
> Nor is there any escape. Long ago this was dear to
> Zeus and the son of Zeus who strikes from afar who

Leon Golden

> earlier willingly protected me. Now, however, my
> fate has descended on me. May I not perish without
> a struggle and ingloriously but may I perform some
> great deed that generations to come will learn of."
> (22.300-05)

Hector has always known that it is glory that must sustain and justify him. Nothing in Andromache's touching appeal to him in book 6 which raises the specter of pathetic suffering to come for those he loves the most, not even holding and comforting his frightened son in his arms, sways him from the determination to seek lasting honor, no matter what the cost.

At the core of the heroic code, as we have seen, is the willingness to risk life, which is fragile, limited in duration, and in the symbolism of the theology of the *Iliad*, a depressingly trivial matter *sub specie aeternitatis* for the reward of enduring commemoration of an act of courage that will be recognized by generations to come. To satisfy grudges and to maintain an uncontested control of the world, the gods, we have seen, are willing with easy consciences, to trade off their favorite cities for destruction; heroic code heroes are ready and willing, *if necessary*, to trade off their temporal survival for permanent existence in the honored memories of mankind. What makes the *Iliad* such a powerful study of the human condition is its persuasive realism and that is why I have emphasized the phrase, *if necessary*, when referring to the willingness of heroic code heroes to risk their lives for glory. For there is one influential view abroad about the relationship of Homeric heroes to death that seriously undercuts the realism of the poem and demeans the nature of the sacrifice warriors are willing to make. This view is the "beautiful death" theory of J.-P. Vernant.[20] Let us get at the essence of his argument:

> The gods have so arranged it that the human
> condition is not only mortal but also, like all earthly
> life after its youthful efflorescence, subject to the
> debilitating effects of age. Heroic striving has
> its roots in the will to escape aging and death,
> however "inevitable" they may be, and leave them
> both behind. Death is overcome when it is made

Understanding the Iliad

welcome instead of being merely experienced...
(57)

What is troubling in Vernant's comment and is ultimately quite wrong in terms of the Homeric world view is his assertion that the essential goal of the Homeric hero, the very act of "heroic striving" is inspired by the "will to escape aging and death" and that the Homeric hero accomplishes this by making death "welcome." Vernant goes even further than this in insisting that the hero's death in battle provides him with "eternal youth" and makes him "immune to aging":

> To pass by death is also to escape the process of aging....Growing old means that one must watch the fabric of life gradually, becoming frayed, damaged, torn by the same power of destruction...that leads to death....To fall on the battlefield saves the warrior from such inexorable decay, such deterioration of all the virtues that comprise masculine *aretê*. Heroic death seizes the fighter when he is... completely intact in the integrity of a vital power still untouched by any decrepitude. He will haunt the memory of men to come in whose eyes his death has secured him in the luster of ideal youth. Thus the *kleos aphthiton* [imperishable glory] the hero gains through his early death also opens to him the path to eternal youth....In the imperishable glory conferred on him by the song about his deeds, he becomes immune to aging in the same way that, as much as it is humanly possible, he escapes the destruction of death. (59-60)

Now, while there is, of course, evidence that Homeric heroes will choose death over dishonor, there is no evidence at all that these heroes—including Achilles, Hector, and Sarpedon—ever *welcome* death, ever go out of their way to court it promiscuously, ever choose Vernant's "beautiful death" over survival with honor. I will go on to show that death is anything but "welcome" to the Homeric heroes, and that the desire to stay alive is a fundamental motivation for them. Those who do survive combat, such as Ajax, Diomedes, and Odysseus are not pejoratively described as having

Leon Golden

failed in their mission to achieve eternal youth; nor are those, like Nestor, who long before were immersed in war and have lived to tell the tale, regarded as pathetic victims of the decrepitude of old age but, rather, viewed with honor and respect and treated with piety. A commentary on dying young in battle that rings much truer than Vernant's thesis is one which Bernard Knox, distinguished classicist and combat veteran of the Spanish Civil War and World War II, offers in recollection of the emotions he felt when he realized that he might die from a serious wound he had sustained in fighting around Madrid:[21]

> I was consumed with rage—furious, violent rage. Why me? I was just 21 and had barely begun living my life. Why should I have to die? It was unjust. And, as I felt my whole being sliding into nothingness, I cursed. I cursed God and the world and everyone in it as the darkness fell.
> Many years later, when I returned to the study of the ancient classics, I found that my reaction was not abnormal. In Homer's *Iliad*, still the greatest of war books, this is how young men die. Hector, for example, "went winging down to the House of Death/wailing his fate, leaving his manhood far behind, his young and supple strength." And Virgil's Turnus goes the same road: *vitaque cum gemitu fugit indignata sub umbras*: "his life with a groan fled angry to the shades below." *Indignata. Quia iuvenis erat*, the great Virgilian commentator explained. "Angry. Because he was young."

Bernard Knox found himself in the same position as Homeric warriors who were dying young in combat and his real-world reaction was "rage—furious, violent rage" at the prospect of an early death, not joy in defeating the pain and sorrow of old age. This actual experience of a young soldier facing death should give us pause in assessing Vernant's view, but the "beautiful death" thesis crumbles totally in the face of one critical word in Homer's description of the departure of Hector's life to the House of Death "*WAILING* his fate." (Emphasis mine.) Mourning, lament, and grief are the emotions Homer evokes from us by the term "wailing" and the lament is directed at the tragedy of Hector's yielding his

Understanding the Iliad

young manhood up to death (as Virgil understood so well in his paraphrase of the Homeric line).

The relationship of the Homeric heroes to death has been treated very perceptively by Robert Renehan and his conclusions come into serious conflict with the beautiful death thesis that privileges early death at the height of one's youth and manhood as the greatest act of heroism possible in the context of Homeric warfare.[22] First of all, Renehan challenges the centrality of the heroic death theme in the *Iliad.* He points out that Homer provides a description of the deaths of three great heroes—Patroclus, Sarpedon, and Hector—but of these three only Sarpedon's death, he argues, is truly heroic. In regard to Patroclus, Renehan notes that he is first described as being stunned by Apollo, then wounded in the back by Euphorbos before he is slain by Hector. During this time, Renehan states (109), Patroclus attempts to avoid death ("Homer is explicit on this") by shrinking back "into the throng of his fellow warriors." It is at this point that Hector slays him and Renehan pointedly asks "how a warrior who is killed while he is running away in an attempt to save his own life can be said to have died defiantly and heroically—looking death in the face, as it were—is not readily apparent."

Hector, the great hero of Troy, also demonstrates to us no driving commitment for a "beautiful death" in the sense that Vernant uses the term. Nor does he, like a number of other Homeric heroes, illustrate *unconditionally* the heroic code mandate for which Schein states "there is no real alternative" that "to be fully human—that is, to be a hero—means to kill or be killed for honor and glory." In book 20, 375-80 we have a narrative use of a god's action to shape the movement of the plot and also an example of strongly implied double motivation on the divine and human levels:

> Phoebus Apollo spoke standing near Hector: "In no
> way any longer be the champion against Achilles
> But await him in the multitude, away from the din
> of War lest he strike you with spear or sword." He
> spoke, and Hector fell back into throng of men
> Terrified, when he heard the god speaking.

One purpose of Apollo's intervention is, of course, to reserve the climactic confrontation between Achilles and Hector for

Leon Golden

book 22, after the explosive power of Achilles's wrath has been demonstrated on the battlefield as preparation for the savage slaughter of Hector and the brutalization of his corpse. The advice that Apollo gives is motivation on the divine level for Hector's actions, but that advice—to wait for Achilles in the throng so as to lessen the chance of being hit by his spear or his sword—also makes excellent sense in human terms for anyone who wanted to stay alive in the face of the maniacal onslaught of Achilles. The fact that Hector unhesitatingly follows this advice tells us that the heroic code mandate "to kill or be killed" can be waived by heroes in favor of the impulse to stay alive and the opportunities for achieving the so-called "beautiful death" may be avoided by them. More evidence for the realistic nature of the heroic code as opposed to romanticized versions comes in book 22. As the threat of Achilles's savage fury draws nearer to Hector, the *first* thought that comes to him is to *barter* for his life with his adversary by laying down his arms and offering an impressive ransom consisting of half the wealth of Troy, in addition to returning Helen and all the possessions she brought with her.

He soon realizes, however, that Achilles's rage is so great that the idea of negotiations with him is pure folly. "Better," he says, "to come together in combat as quickly as possible; let us know to which of the two of us the Olympian will grant glory" (22.129-30). Such an action would reflect what the heroic code dictates, but the fierceness of Achilles's pursuit changes his mind and makes him completely forget the "killing or being killed" ethic of that code. When he caught sight of Achilles's gleaming armor "trembling seized him nor did he dare to remain there but he left gates behind and departed in fear; and the son of Peleus, trusting in his swift feet, flew after him" (22.136-38). Homer describes in some detail the fierce chase around the city until Hector decides to stand and face the onslaught of Achilles. We recall that this takes place *only* after two strategies, bartering for his life and fleeing his enemy, have failed to deflect the climactic "killing or being killed" mandate that would fulfill the requirements of the orthodox heroic code. Hector will certainly choose death now, rather than shame and cowardice, but it is also very clear that his first two impulses in facing Achilles were to privilege *life* over death, "beautiful" or not, and he shares this impulse to survive with Patroclus, as Renehan has pointed out, and with real-world soldiers in combat, as we can infer from Bernard Knox's personal reflections on his emotions

Understanding the Iliad

as he lay seriously wounded on a battlefield. Indeed, the true excellence of the war theme in the *Iliad* is its uncompromising realism, a realism that is betrayed if we accept any form of the romanticized view of the heroic code.

There is much evidence throughout the *Iliad* that *survival and life* are very important factors in the Homeric hero's mind but that at critical moments, for a cause of great importance, they must be sacrificed for the higher value and lasting achievement of winning enduring *glory* that has the power to defeat the pathos of the human condition. Renehan's remarks below are an accurate rebuttal of the romanticized view of the heroic code, but not a fair account of the power residing in the *realistic* heroic code to enrich life with meaning:[23]

> It thus appears, remarkably, that heroic death, in the strictest sense of the term, is not particularly prominent in the *Iliad*.... Moreover, despite the modem tendency to write of Homeric warriors "dying a hero's death" and "resolving to die fighting"....the reality is that very often they show fear, panic, and a most definite desire to go on living.

In arguing for a realistic view of the heroic code in the *Iliad,* I most certainly do not wish to demean that code (which is something I believe romanticized interpretations actually accomplish) but to elevate its importance. It is precisely because Homeric heroes *realistically value life over death* that their willingness to *risk* their lives at critical moments is so important and lends grandeur to their role as warriors and genuine significance to their lives. There are an impressive number of incidents in the *Iliad* that affirm a realistic view of the heroic code as opposed to a romanticized one, and I want to survey them now.

In book 2, Agamemnon receives a false dream from Zeus that promises him a victory at Troy. He decides to check on the morale of his army by reporting to them the opposite message, that Zeus has declared that the Achaian army will suffer defeat. He hopes, of course, that the army will rebel against this warning of loss and demonstrate for heroic code or other reasons the will to carry on the attack. He eloquently feigns an expression of despair, emphasizing how long and fruitlessly the Achaians have

Leon Golden

fought against the Trojans, how their ships have rotted as they lay for nine years on the beaches of Ilium, and, most importantly, how painful has been their lengthy separation from wives and children. The army's reaction answers to Agamemnon's worst fears. The men, enticed by the vision of returning home, race to the beach to launch their ships for an immediate return, which is thwarted only by the intervention of Odysseus, who is able to restore military discipline. The rush to the ships is certainly no great advertisement for the romanticized version of the heroic code but it does not subvert the realistic heroic code that operates within the poem. Agamemnon had touched on the two deepest chords of military morale as he called up the specter of military defeat and the siren song of homeward return. Under the pressure of these two powerful forces, the army's rush to the ships is understandable and highly realistic when they are exposed to a prophecy of defeat. At this early point in the poem, we should be aware that the heroic code will not be a prescription for invariable superhuman behavior, but a doctrine that will be applied selectively by human beings for the most part as good as we are or somewhat better in a realistic manner depending on existing circumstances.

No one demonstrates a more capricious attitude toward the heroic code than Paris. His bravado in book 3 in first challenging the Achaian army and then desperately fleeing a fiercely pursuing Menelaus adds no heroic laurels to his reputation and, indeed, book 3 is much more about seduction and sensuality than it is about war and heroism. Paris expresses a cavalier attitude toward his violation of the heroic code in this book by looking forward to another, more favorable occasion in the war, when the gods will be on his side, and then by saying to Helen:

> "Come now, let us go to bed and make love. For never before has love so enfolded my heart, Not when I first took you from lovely Lacedaemon And sailed with you on my seafaring ships, And made love to you on the island of Cranae As now I love you and sweet desire overpowers me." He spoke and led the way to the bed, and his wife followed. (3.441-47)

In book 11, however, we see Paris performing a heroic code role effectively as he wounds with his bow and takes out of action

Understanding the Iliad

three important Achaian warriors: Diomedes, Machaon, and Eurypylus and thus justifies Hector's comment:

> "Strange man no one who is right-minded could
> dishonor your service in battle, since you are a
> strong fighter; but of your own free will you slack
> off—and lack willpower." (6.521-23)

Owen catches some of the idiosyncratic character of Paris when he describes him as "superficially an attractive figure, good-natured, lighthearted, irresponsible—out of place and hence something of a relief among the grimly earnest warriors about him—."[24] In Paris, Homer has given us the most extreme case of a Homeric warrior who is highly selective about his choice of occasions on which he will and will not follow the canon of the heroic code. It is important, however, as justification for privileging the realistic interpretation of the heroic code over romanticized versions, to remain fully aware that other warriors, including Agamemnon and Achilles, like Paris, are selective in choosing when to obey and when not to obey the "killing or being killed" injunction that we have been told is a requirement of the code.

Aeneas, one of the greatest of the Trojan leaders, also has a selective capacity for facing and avoiding danger. In book 5, we are told that he killed two of the best of the Danaans. Just a few lines later, Aeneas faces Menelaus in heroic, one-on-one confrontation:

> The two were holding their hands and sharp spears
> Against each other, eager to fight when Antilochus
> Came and stood by the shepherd of the people. But
> Aeneas, although a swift warrior, did not stand his
> ground, when he saw the two men remaining side
> by side. (5.568-72)

What is on Aeneas's mind here is *survival and life,* not the glory of "killing or being killed" or a "beautiful death."

More evidence that life can be privileged over death by Homeric warriors is seen in the meeting on the battlefield of Glaucus and Diomedes in book 6. In their encounter, Diomedes discovers that old ties of hospitality going back to their grandfathers link the two heroes as guest/friends. Diomedes

Leon Golden

announces that the ties that bind them trump the enmity generated by their being on opposite sides in the war, and cancel any obligation of "killing or being killed" to attain heroic status or a "beautiful death." It is rather a generous continuation of life that they bestow upon each other. Owen has a perceptive understanding of the incident:[25]

> Homer closes the Diomedes episode with the scene of his meeting with Glaucus. The incident is a lovely and pleasant thing in itself. It lights up the field with a sudden gleam of kindliness and the high chivalry that can beautify war. There are still other feelings, we are shown, stronger than the hate that war engenders, than the implacable desire for revenge that Agamemnon has just given expression to; the sanctity of other relationships can overrule the bitter relationship of foe with foe. The point is established in our minds without perhaps our particularly noticing it, but who is to say that it has not its soothing effect in the bitter developments that are to come? There is, as it were, a promise, the suggestion of a hope, stored in the mind, waiting for fulfillment.

In the gracious, life-affirming actions of Diomedes and Glaucus here we detect a foreshadowing of the humane, life-affirming event that brings the *Iliad* to its climax, the reconciliation that takes place between Achilles and Priam in book 24.

In book 7, another event occurs that, at two separate levels, privileges *survival and life* over the "kill or be killed" ethic associated with the orthodox heroic code. Hector issues a challenge for one-on-one combat with any Achaian warrior who is willing to volunteer for the opportunity of winning or giving the greatest of glory. Although the heroic code rewards are so very great in this offer of a direct encounter with Hector, initially the Achaians were silent, and afraid to accept (7.92-93). Finally Menelaus, disgusted with the inaction of his comrades steps forward to answer Hector's challenge, although we are told he was sure to lose his life in the encounter because Hector was by far the stronger fighter. The Achaian commanders intervene, however, and Agamemnon says:

Understanding the Iliad

> "You are mad, Zeus-nurtured Menelaus, There is
> no need for this folly of yours. Restrain yourself
> although you are troubled and do not be willing in
> rivalry to fight a better man than you, Priam's son
> Hector, whom others also fear and even Achilles
> shudders to meet him in battle which brings glory
> to men and he is a far better warrior than you. But
> you go now and sit down among the band of your
> comrades. Against this man the Achaians will raise
> up another champion." (7.109-16)

Agamemnon and the Greek commanders will not allow
Menelaus to pursue heroic code glory in an uneven struggle that
he cannot win, and in which he must lose his life. They place
a greater value on Menelaus's *survival and life* than on futile
heroics that will lead to death. With Menelaus protected, and after
an appeal by Nestor, lots are drawn to see who will be Hector's
opponent, and the choice falls on Ajax. The explicit conditions set
for the encounter by Hector are precisely those of the orthodox
heroic code: *to kill or be killed.* The loser in this deadly match
would achieve Vernant's "beautiful death" for, as Hector says, he
will be killed "in his prime" and the winner will walk away with the
heroic code's greatest of honors for his fame "will not die." The
struggle begins and is fierce between the two great heroes, until
a boulder hurled by Ajax drops Hector to his knees. From this
powerful blow, he rises up again and both are ready to continue
the fight to the death that Hector had ordained, except that the
heralds, Talthybius and Idaeus, intervene and stand between the
two strong fighters. Idaeus then urges both of them:

> "My two sons, fight and battle no longer. Zeus, the
> cloud gatherer, loves both of you and you are both
> spearmen, which we all know. It is already night
> and it is good to obey night." (7.279-82)

Ajax demands that Hector state this offer in his own words
and that if he does so he will agree to a cessation of the struggle.
Hector does ask for a truce and then suggests:

Leon Golden

> "But let us both give glorious gifts to each other so
> that some Greek and Trojan will say of us: 'Both of
> them fought each other in soul-devouring strife, and
> then agreed to part in friendship.'" (7.299-302)

There is joy in Troy and in the Achaian camp as both heroes return to their people; and once again, a life-affirming and life-preserving ethic overcomes the "kill or be killed" dictates of the orthodox heroic code and foreshadows the climactic victory of humane values that will take place in the encounter between Achilles and Priam in book 24.

We have seen that Menelaus was prevented from foolishly becoming a sacrifice to the requirements of the orthodox heroic code in book 7, where defeat for him would have been inevitable. In book 8, we have an illuminating event in which—under the same heroic code conditions—Diomedes and Odysseus make contradictory decisions at a critical moment in regard to their obligations to fulfilling the orthodox mandates of the code. Here the tide of the battle has turned to the Trojan side. Idomeneus, Agamemnon, and the two Ajaxes are all put to flight. Nestor alone remains, unwillingly, in a vulnerable position because Paris had seriously wounded one of his horses. The situation becomes critical for him as Hector comes rapidly in pursuit eager for the kill. It is at this point that:

> ...the old man would have lost his life there If
> Diomedes, good at the war-cry had not kept a
> sharp watch. He shouted a terrifying cry urging
> Odysseus into action: "wily, Zeus-born, son of
> Laertes, where are you fleeing, turning your back
> like a coward in the ranks. May someone not fix a
> spear in your back as you flee. But stand firm so
> that we may drive this wild warrior away from the
> old man." Thus he spoke but much-enduring, noble
> Odysseus didn't hear or didn't heed but darted by
> to the hollow ships of the Achaians. Nevertheless,
> Diomedes, although he was alone, stood in front of
> all before the horses of the old man. (8.90-100)

Diomedes's actions here fit the letter and word of the orthodox heroic code, but Odysseus's conduct has stunned the many

Understanding the Iliad

commentators who have not realized how prominent behavior in accordance with the *realistic,* as opposed to the *romanticized* code, is in this poem. Willcock, for example, cannot believe that Homer would describe the hero Odysseus as less brave than his status demanded and, since the Greek word representing Odysseus's failure to "hear" or "heed" Diomedes's call for aid is ambiguous, he prefers to think that in this instance Odysseus suffers "from a temporary deafness."[26] Kirk comments that interpreting the text as meaning that Odysseus did not "heed" Diomedes "would make his behaviour positively disgraceful" and goes so far as to suggest some kind of textual corruption in this passage in order to avoid such an interpretation.[27] We have seen, however, that there is considerable evidence that Homeric heroes can and do choose to pursue *survival and life* rather than glory and a "beautiful" death.

If Odysseus, in this instance, focuses his attention on the escape from death, then he does nothing that clashes with the conduct of the great Trojan hero, Aeneas, earlier in the poem, or with the even greater Trojan hero, Hector, later, as he awaits the onslaught of Achilles. If we realize that it is a mark of Homer's skill that his depiction of soldiers at war is not superficially romantic but, rather, highly realistic, emotionally and psychologically, then we will not need to have recourse to devices such as "temporary deafness" or "textual interpolation" to explain Odysseus's impulse to stay alive in the passage under discussion. The *Iliad* is an insightful, truthful mimesis of human action precisely because it is dedicated to contemplating, with penetrating clarity, what lies both on the surface and in the shadows of the heroic psyche. It is not only Paris, but heroes of the stature of Hector, Aeneas, and Patroclus, *even Achilles* (although he is a much more complex case) who will at times choose *life and survival* over the opportunity for enduing glory that might require a heroic death.

Agamemnon is a military leader with a clearly variable attitude toward the heroic code. In book 4, for example, we learn that Agamemnon exercises his leadership responsibilities fully in tune with heroic code dictates. After Menelaus is wounded in battle, we learn that:

> Then you would not have seen noble Agamemnon
> sleeping or cowering or unwilling to fight but very
> eager for battle where men win glory. (4.223-25)

Leon Golden

We see a very different Agamemnon in book 9 where, deeply discouraged about the prospects for military success, he says:

> "Come now, as I command let us all obey. Let us
> flee with our ships to our dear native land; For there
> is no way that we shall still capture Troy's wide
> streets." (9.26-28)

The reaction to this pronouncement is of great interest. Diomedes arises to condemn this defeatist call for retreat in the face of failure and he gains the support of the rest of the Achaian chieftains for his position. Agamemnon yields to the countervailing judgments of his officers and his initial willingness to abandon the heroic code does not bring about revolt or vituperation. Rather, Nestor suggests that a Council of Leaders be summoned to discuss strategy and notes that Agamemnon's alienation of Achilles is responsible for their plight. Agamemnon accepts responsibility for his actions and promises to atone for them by awarding an impressive inventory of gifts to Achilles. Thus, in spite of Agamemnon's willingness to betray the central tenet of the orthodox heroic code—the obligation to attain glory by killing or being killed—he retains his authority. In book 11.91-279 Agamemnon returns to orthodox heroic code form as he performs in a spirited way, as a ferocious warrior, killing many of his opponents on the battlefield. Yet in book 14, we see a despondent and pessimistic Agamemnon urging retreat and unheroic flight to safety again:

> "Let us drag all of the ships drawn up first near the
> Sea, draw them all into the bright sea, and moor
> Them afloat with anchor stones until immortal
> night comes, if indeed the Trojans desist from war
> Because of her. Then we might drag down all the
> Ships. For it is not a cause for resentment to flee
> Disaster, even by night. Better to flee and escape
> than to be seized by it." (14.75-81)

Odysseus and Diomedes strongly object to this counsel of despair, and Agamemnon changes his position and accedes to Diomedes's advice for handling the current trouble in which the

Understanding the Iliad

Achaian army finds itself. We must emphasize that in spite of the fact Agamemnon has acted initially in a way that contradicts the orthodox heroic code, he retains his authority as commander-in-chief. What we learn from Agamemnon's role in the poem is that great variability in the application of the mandates of the heroic code, reflecting the realism of actual combat, is tolerated.

I have been emphasizing that to understand the true nature of heroic activity in the *Iliad,* we must recognize the authenticity with which Homer describes it and not be diverted by romanticized interpretations of that heroic behavior. This is not to deny, and we should not omit notice and valuation of those events, and there are a number, that are interspersed in the action of the poem which are fully in accord with the heroic code principle of "killing or being killed." Agamemnon's bravery and effectiveness as a warrior in book 11, where he kills one Trojan fighter after another, is certainly an impressive example of such an event. The dangerous espionage mission undertaken by Diomedes and Odysseus in book 10, carried out by them with verve, skill, and bravery is another such example. The total picture of warfare in the *Iliad* which Homer gives us is a complex tapestry of events that range from the heroic willingness to kill or be killed of the heroes cited above to the depressing cowardice and betrayal of his own forces by Dolon in book 10 and the deep pathos of young soldiers dying too soon or too unluckily to attain even a modicum of glory. Most important to remember is that Homer portrays the realism—not the fantasy—of war and that there is no contradiction in the fact that warriors capable of great heroism in combat, also privilege *survival and life* over death. This important aspect of realistic heroic code activity, the willingness to kill or be killed *and* the privileging of *survival and life* over death, can be seen with precision in book 11 in Hector's encounter with Diomedes and Odysseus. As Hector charges the two Achaian chieftains, Diomedes calls to Odysseus:

> "Let us stand firm awaiting him and ward him off."
> He spoke, and brandishing his far-shadowing spear,
> he hurled it, and did not miss his aim but struck him
> on the head on the top of the helmet. But bronze
> was driven aside by bronze and did not reach his
> beautiful skin.... and Hector swiftly ran back an
> impressive distance and kept within the crowd.
> He fell on his knees and stayed there and with his

Leon Golden

> stout hand he leaned upon the earth. Dark night
> covered over his eyes. Then Diomedes rushed after
> his spear far through the foremost fighters where it
> had gone down in the earth and meanwhile Hector
> regained his breath and rushing back to his chariot
> he drove into the crowd and avoided a dark fate.
> (11.348-60)

In this single incident, Diomedes plays the role of a hero ready to kill or be killed as he withstands the onslaught of Hector, while Hector plays the role of a hero who chooses *survival and life* as he faces uneven odds (Diomedes *and* Odysseus). Both, however, are genuine heroes and fully obedient to the realistic heroic code of the epic.

We noted an event in book 8 when Odysseus, privileging *survival and life,* raced to safety, not heeding Diomedes's call for aid in defending Nestor. In book 11, we observe very different behavior on the part of Odysseus. He finds himself left alone on the battlefield since the other Greek warriors had fled. Here he ponders his alternatives:

> "Alas, what will happen to me? It is a calamity if I
> flee, terrified by their host but it is more fearful If I
> am captured all alone since Zeus has driven the
> rest of the Danaans into flight. But why does my
> heart debate with me about this? For I know that
> cowards depart from war but he that is pre-eminent
> in battle, must stand firm whether he strikes another
> or is himself struck down." (11.404-10)

Odysseus then goes on the offensive against the Trojans until they turn against him in numbers and he has to shout for help from his comrades. Menelaus hears the alarm and says to Telemonian Ajax:

> "Ajax, the cry of steadfast Odysseus reaches me. It
> is likely that the Trojans have cut him off all alone in
> the savage battle. Let us traverse the host for it is
> better to save him. I fear what he may suffer alone
> among the Trojans, Brave as he is—a man we
> would miss." (11.465-71)

Understanding the Iliad

Two important points are made in this passage about the realistic heroic code as opposed to the orthodox or romanticized versions of it. Odysseus, in book 8, when he flees the battlefield seeking to preserve his life, and in book 11, when he risks his life in circumstances involving killing and being killed is the *same* authentic, realistic hero. We must understand the realistic proposition that in Homeric warfare and, in warfare in general, courageous warriors will, under certain conditions, privilege *survival and life* over death and, under other conditions, fully expose themselves to the risks of killing or being killed. Secondly, we should note that Menelaus and Ajax have no intention of allowing Odysseus to find any kind of death, including the so-called "beautiful death" in battle. Further, Odysseus in this scene also has not the slightest intention of yielding himself up to death, for Homer tells us:

> The Trojans, many and powerful, pursued
> Odysseus, skilful and warlike, from every Direction
> but the great fighter maneuvering Swiftly with his
> spear warded off the day Of his doom. (11.482-84)

From this point on, battles rage until the climactic encounter between Achilles and Hector is reached. In the these life-and-death conflicts, and especially in the encounters between Hector and Patroclus and Achilles and Hector, Homer provides us with ample opportunities to observe both sides of the realistic heroic code, the aspiration for winning glory by killing or being killed, as well as the strong impulse for *survival and life*.

Further confirmation that the realistic heroic code encompasses the choice of *survival and life* occurs in book 16, where Hector is on the point of defeating Ajax who then retreated, out of the way of the missiles (16.122). Later, in book 16, with Zeus serving as a narrative agent, Hector turns to flight and calls on the rest of the Trojans to flee in the fierce combat around Sarpedon's corpse (16.656.58). There is no suggestion here of any inappropriateness in Hector's act of self-preservation in preference to involvement in killing or being killed and no indication that Hector has destroyed his status as a hero by his defection from the battlefield at this point. At the climax of book 16, it is Patroclus's time to die. It takes two human adversaries to finish

Leon Golden

him off; the first, Euphorbus, inflicts a serious wound but not a fatal one and leaves it to Hector to strike the death blow. Euphorbus's assault sends Patroclus running back to his allies and taking protective cover with them (11.816-17). Hector then pursues him and takes his life. Once again, there is no suggestion in the text of condemnation of Patroclus in heroic code terms for seeking safety after Euphorbus's attack rather than the reward of glory emanating from "killing or being killed" or of welcoming a so-called "beautiful death." In book 17, one of the best illustrations we have of the way in which considerations of *survival and life* interact with orthodox heroic code goals occurs when Menelaus ponders his dilemma in defending the corpse of Patroclus from the pursuing Trojans:

> "Ah me, if I abandon the beautiful armor and Patroclus too, who lies here for my honor, May no one of the Danaans be angry at me who sees it. But, if, alone, I fight Hector and the Trojans out of shame, I fear that many will surround me, when I am by myself....No Danaan will be angry who sees me retreating before Hector who fights with gods at his side. But if I could see somewhere Ajax known for his mighty war cry both of us might go back and think of the joy of battle even against the will of the gods. If only we might save the corpse for Achilles, son of Peleus. That is the best of the evils that face us." (17.91-105)

Here, perfectly balanced against each other, are the two principles of the realistic heroic code of the *Iliad*: the willingness to *risk* one's life for honor and enduring glory and the rational commitment to *survival and life* of the soldier in combat.

I have already mentioned the events involved in the climactic scene of combat in the poem, Hector's encounter with Achilles in book 22. Here Hector ponders achieving *survival and life* by offering a huge ransom for his own safety, then flees to save his life when he judges his offer to be a totally unacceptable proposition to the raging Achilles and then, and only then, does he accept the orthodox heroic code mandate of "killing or being killed." Once again, there is no suggestion in the text that Hector's initial choice of *survival and life* is destructive of his role as a hero. No less a judge of courage than Achilles is the custodian

Understanding the Iliad

of Hector's honor as he, willingly and without reservation, affirms Hector's heroic stature and provides for his glorification in death through the sumptuous funeral he allows to take place for him in book 24. This act of magnanimity toward a fallen enemy insures as well the soaring elevation of the stature of Achilles, himself.

I have argued that the realistic heroic code of the epic supplies values to the life and death of human beings that are a potent weapon against meaninglessness. That code offers the attainment of enduring glory as compensation for the grim and savage deaths that overtake many in warfare. Not everyone, however, who goes to war, Homer knows, successfully participates in the rewards of the realistic heroic code. The poet has peopled his armies, quite realistically, with many who—too soon and too unluckily—perish without the opportunity of earning the accolades of courage and glory that would invest their lives with significance. Those who die this way, without any achievement that offers enduring glory as a reward, contribute a large measure of pathos to the emotional effect of the *Iliad*. This theme has been treated comprehensively and definitively by Jasper Griffin.[28]

I want to conclude this chapter with a discussion of four important examples of the deep pathos that arises from death in war, to which Homer awards no heroic code honor but, rather, envelops that death in an atmosphere of sorrow for the sad waste of human life. In book 4, Ajax kills Simoeisius, and the description goes as follows:

> His mother bore him going down from Ida by the
> banks of Simois when she followed her parents to
> see their flocks. For that reason they called him
> Simoeisius. But he did not repay his dear parents
> the cost of his rearing for his life was brief. He was
> overpowered by the spear of great-hearted Ajax
> who struck him on the right breast by the nipple as
> he advanced in the front ranks. And straight through
> the shoulder the bronze spear went. He fell to the
> ground in the dust like a poplar tree. (4.474-82)

This description belongs to a number that Griffin has usefully designated as "obituaries" in that they communicate some important aspects of the life of the dead soldier. We learn something about his parents, the circumstances under which he

Leon Golden

was born, and, most importantly, that he was very young and died before he could accomplish anything of value in his life. When he is slain, he is not engaged in heroic combat against another powerful warrior which could earn him glory, even in death, for we are told that Ajax killed him as he strode amid the front lines of his army prior to a direct confrontation with a hero that could have yielded him heroic code rewards. Most pathetic of all in this obituary is the line referring to his parents, that he died before he could pay them back the cost of rearing him. This emphasizes the utter waste of his own lost life, dying young without significant achievement, and the profound desolation in the lives of parents who will never see him again and who thought so much of him that they had given him a name that would forever remind them of the place of his birth.

In book 8, Teucer has his eye on Hector as a target:

> And he sent another arrow from his string straight
> At Hector and he longed to hit him, however he
> Missed him but struck noble Gorgythion, the brave
> Son of Priam, in the breast with an arrow. A woman
> Priam wed from Aesyme gave birth to him, lovely
> Castianeira, who resembled a goddess in beauty.
> And he bent his head to one side like a poppy in
> a Garden that is weighed down with its fruit and
> Springtime rains. Thus his head, heavy in his
> Helmet, sank to one side. (8. 300-08)

In this obituary, we learn of the parentage of Gorgythion and specifically of the beauty of his mother, one of Priam's concubines. But most important we learn that his death was an accident of war; Teucer was aiming at Hector and missed and struck Gorgythion. He won no glory from combat, one on one, that could lead to a glorious act of the killing and being killed variety; he was merely in the wrong place at the wrong time. To the pathos of his meaningless death is added the sadness of the simile that compares the sagging head of the dying soldier sunk into his wounded and bleeding chest with the rich red hue of a flower gathering its vital force in the rains of springtime. Gorgythion's death is another waste of human life without the compensation of heroic code rewards.

Understanding the Iliad

In book 11, another deep note of pathos is sounded in the death of Iphidamas, who has the opportunity to engage in a heroic code encounter, unlike Simoeisius and Gorgythion, but one that fails to erase the pathos of his death. Of Iphidamas we are told:

> Cisseus raised him in his house from early youth
> The father of his mother, Theano....And when he
> reached his glorious youth, He tried to keep him
> there by offering him his own daughter in marriage.
> But Iphidamas after he married her departed from
> The marriage chamber in pursuit of the report of the
> Coming of the Achaeans... (11.223-27)

In his confrontation with Agamemnon, Iphidamas drives his spear toward his opponent's stomach, but Agamemnon's defensive armor deflects it. Then:

> Agamemnon struck him on the neck with His sword
> and unstrung his limbs. And the fallen Iphidamas
> slept the sleep of bronze, Pitiable man, helping
> his fellow citizens, far from His wedded wife, from
> whom he had known no joy, but had given much
> for her, First, A hundred head of cattle, and then
> he promised a thousand goats and sheep together,
> Those tended for him in his countless herds.
> Then Agamemnon, the son of Atreus, stripped his
> Fine armor and carried it through the host of the
> Achaians. (11.240-47)

In spite of the fact that Iphidamas has achieved the orthodox heroic code reward that comes from killing or being killed in combat, Homer impresses several layers of pathos on this scene. First, there is the attempt by his family to keep him safe at home out of the war. Then there is his marriage immediately prior to leaving for the hostilities at Troy and the fact that he suffered an early death at Agamemnon's hands when he entered the struggle and "slept a sleep of bronze." Finally, there is Homer's reflection on the marriage that had brought him no joy, although he had paid much for his bride. Since Iphidamas acted with the bravery of a heroic code warrior in confronting Agamemnon, Homer had the opportunity to emphasize the honor that comes from dying

Leon Golden

courageously in battle. It is of great interest that he chooses here to stress the pathetic emptiness and loss involved in Iphidamas's death.

The final incident of this type that I wish to cite concerns the death of Polydorus, Priam's youngest son, at the hands of Achilles in book 20. We are told:

> Achilles went next after god-like Polydorus, Priam's
> son. His father would not allow him to fight at all,
> since he was the youngest and dearest among
> his children. His swiftness was very great but,
> foolishly showing off his skill, he rushed through
> the foremost ranks, until he lost his life. As he
> darted by, swift-footed, God-like Achilles, struck him
> with his spear in the middle of his back where the
> golden fastenings of his belt closed and the twofold
> breastplate came together. And straight Through
> beside the navel the spear-point held its Way.
> He fell to his knees screaming and a dark Cloud
> covered him over. He grasped his bowels in His
> hands as he sank to the ground. (20.407-18)

We can tell in this passage how central Polydorus is in the affections of the great king, his father, as the youngest of his sons. Priam would not allow him to fight, but the youthful Polydorus is foolishly eager to demonstrate his great speed of foot, and Achilles strikes him, fatally, as he races by. The grim details of the lethal wound announce the termination of a young life which achieved no heroic code reward for the foolish daring that was shown. Along with the painful demise of the boy, we sense the profound grief of the father for his youngest son.

I have tried to show in this chapter that the anthropomorphic gods of the *Iliad* symbolize impersonal forces always at work in the universe—fate, chance, historical necessity—that are outside of human control and operate capriciously and often to the detriment of human happiness and aspirations. Sarpedon reminds Glaucus that death abounds in many forms, and because of that inescapable reality and, in the absence of any guarantees offered by natural or supernatural forces, the burden rests completely on mankind to make something of value of both life and death in order to avoid the fate of "the mass of men" [who], in the philosopher

Understanding the Iliad

Thoreau's words "lead lives of quiet desperation." The orthodox heroic code is the dominant mechanism in the poem for creating a value system that, for many, accomplishes this goal by offering enduring glory as a reward for the courageous risking of life. Thus war becomes, in an ironic way, an instrument for achieving meaningful life for mankind but it is not the sole mechanism nor the most important one for this purpose in the poem. The most profound form of heroism in the *Iliad*, and the most significant victory won against the play of random forces in the universe, does not emerge from the orthodox heroic code activity of killing and being killed but from quite a different source in the heart, mind, and spirit of Achilles.

Chapter 2

Achilles

The events which unfold in the *Iliad* occur within a fifty-one day period during the ninth year of the Trojan War. Neither the beginning nor the ending of the war take place during this period, although Homer has skillfully integrated much of the larger Trojan War narrative into what has come to be called the *Achilleid*, the specific and more narrowly focused account of Achilles, which he has made the central theme of his poem.[1] It is clear, however, that Homer did not expend any of his considerable poetic brilliance in unifying the action of his poem on the basis of this larger Trojan War story. We know, of course, that there has been disagreement over the long history of the interpretation of the *Iliad* about the poem's unity. Yet, as Aristotle has told us, unity of action is a requirement for excellence in a work of art and I believe that Joachim Latacz expresses a view that is widely accepted today when he says:[2]

> The Iliad exhibits a thoroughly premeditated unity from first to last: there are no overlappings, no actual reduplications, no lapses in logic, no inconsistencies in the basic plan. If one were to ask the *Iliad* poet whether he (like his modern interpreters) had paid special attention to this and whether he had taken special pains to achieve this, he would have likely reacted with surprise. He was preoccupied with creating not a unified epic—that

Understanding the Iliad

was a given—but one that would make the world
more comprehensible and more beautiful (italics
mine).

If we also agree with Latacz, then we must ask what it is that does create unity of action in the fifty-one-day period covered by the story as it is told in the poem. The theme of the first book of the epic is the genesis of the wrath of Achilles, and the subject of the last book focuses on the termination of that wrath and its transformation into compassion. Thus, the events that unfold in book 1 and those that take place in book 24, while very different in their emotional tone, nevertheless provide the unifying theme of the *Iliad* (always remembering that the poem is in structure and scope an *Achilleid*) since they represent the first stage and the last stage of the construction of Achilles's character in the poem. We have, then, a beginning of the poem in book 1 that clearly explicates the source of Achilles's wrath in his quarrel with Agamemnon and an ending in book 24 that demonstrates how that wrath is transformed into compassion as a consequence of the profound effect on Achilles of his moving encounter with Priam. To establish the existence of unity of action in the poem, therefore, means to demonstrate (in Aristotelian terms) the fact that the events of the middle of the story provide a necessary and probable vehicle for the evolution of wrath into compassion.[3]

In the twenty-four books of the *Iliad* which narrate the fifty-one-day period depicted in the poem, Achilles, alone of all the Homeric heroes, is present throughout either in person, as he is in book 1 and book 24 or in his effect on the action of the intermediary books, where he is sometimes present in person and sometimes present through the influence he exerts, in and by, his physical absence. It is an axiom of my interpretation that the *Iliad* is a unified work because of the centrality of Achilles's role in the epic and that we should view all other aspects of the poem from the vantage point of how they shed light, directly or indirectly, on the fate of the *Iliad's* principal character.

At the core, then, of the *Iliad* is an *Achilleid*, a story which will turn out to be, in my analysis, much more a *Bildungsroman*, a story of psychological, moral, and spiritual evolution, than of war. Not every critic has perceived the dominant psychological motif in Homer's portrayal of Achilles. Here are two valuable comments:

39

Leon Golden

> Indeed, the *Iliad* commences not with the whole person "Akhilleus" but with the designation of a state of mind—to wit, "wrath"....We see here an announcement not of the story of a noble hero, and his deeds but of the inner condition of a human being and its effects. The interest is not so much in what the man does but what transpires within him (and forms the basis for his action). It has rightly been suggested that we are witnessing a process of "internalizing" and a tendency to "psychologize" the facts of the sage.[4]

> The first word [of the poem] ('wrath,' 'anger') shows that the plot of the *Iliad* is to be primarily psychological, and that we do not have here a simple chronicle of the fighting at Troy.[5]

I plan to focus in my analysis on the psychological, emotional, and spiritual factors that define Achilles's status as a man and hero, and so we must begin, as the epic itself begins, with his anger, a not at all inappropriate emotion because of Agamemnon's failure to fulfill his command responsibilities by taking action against a plague that is assaulting a helpless army. At first, Achilles's anger is under control, only simmering with a subordinate's complaint that his commander-in-chief does not take control of a situation that is destructive to the army; but then it grows into an all-consuming wrath under the arrogant and irresponsible provocation by Agamemnon that breaks through the thin barriers of his own self-control into a blazing conflagration of hatred until it reaches its climax in a death wish against the army's commander and those, once his allies, who have sided with him. The genesis of the quarrel in book 1 is well known. The priest, Chryses, offers a generous ransom for the daughter Agamemnon has taken from him as a prize and prays as follows:

> "Sons of Atreus and you other well-greaved Achaians May the gods who have Olympian homes Grant you the sacking of Priam's city, and safe return home. But release my daughter to me and accept this ransom In reverence for Zeus' son, Apollo who strikes from afar." (1.17-21)

Understanding the Iliad

The army is pleased with the offer Chryses makes but Agamemnon with inhumane harshness curtly dismisses him with the sneering comment that his daughter will be an "old woman in Argos" before he lets her go and he warns Chryses to leave the camp while he can depart safely. The priest then beseeches Apollo to punish the Achaians for their mistreatment of him and the army, as a result, is afflicted by a plague of death that rains down on it for nine days. In the absence of any action by Agamemnon, Achilles calls an assembly to deal with the disaster and proposes that a priest be consulted who could interpret the cause of Apollo's anger at the army. Here are Achilles's words:

> "Son of Atreus, now I think that we will return home,
> Wandering back, if indeed we should escape
> death, If war and pestilence together will defeat the
> Achaians. But let us ask some prophet or priest or
> an interpreter of dreams, for dreams, indeed, come
> from Zeus, who might tell us why Phoebus Apollo
> is so greatly angered, whether he finds fault with a
> vow or sacrifice and if he would accept the savor
> of unblemished lambs and goats and be willing to
> ward off this plague from us." (1.59-67)

Achilles's suggestion is made respectfully and there is no hint of defiance or condemnation in his request. At this point, the prophet, Calchas, volunteers to speak out but requests protection because he knows that what he has to say will anger Agamemnon, and Achilles is quick to offer the desired security and mentions that it is a blanket commitment of safety for Chalkas against anyone who would threaten him, even if that person be the commander-in-chief, Agamemnon himself. Some readers have seen in Achilles's mention of Agamemnon's name "an aggressive initiative" that could be considered a provocation by Agamemnon,[6] and others think the addition of Agamemnon's name here is a "gratuitous addition" that is "mildly insulting, the beginning of trouble."[7] This would place blame for starting the quarrel on Achilles, but there are good reasons to think that this is not so and that the initial culpability for the dissension here rests with Agamemnon. We have seen that Achilles makes his request that the aid of a priest be sought in the absence of

Leon Golden

any action by Agamemnon to protect the army from unceasing fatalities. If Achilles were looking for an opportunity to provoke Agamemnon, he could easily charge him with dereliction of duty for his failure to intervene in the disaster overwhelming the army or charge him with mad folly (a crime that Agamemnon admits to later for different reasons) for the irresponsible and brutally harsh treatment of Apollo's priest against the wishes of the army which we have noted. Achilles's behavior here, on the contrary, is quite temperate and respectful; it is Chalkas who raises the question of his own personal safety, and the Chryses incident would certainly justify his concern. In guaranteeing his assistance to Chalkas, no matter who might threaten him, Achilles simply assures that the purpose of the assembly he has called—finding a means for protecting the army—will be fulfilled. It is thus Latacz, I think, who understands best what the situation is at this point before open hostility between Achilles and Agamemnon breaks out. He writes concerning the actions of Achilles and Chalkas:[8]

> Is there not at work here an unspoken alliance between thoughtful persons who have the best interests of the group at heart? Persons who know from long experience the volatile temper of their leader, so obstinately proud of his position of supreme authority, and who wish unobtrusively to guide him back onto the right path? To achieve this, someone must say what the misguided individual would never recognize or admit on his own.

If we take this position, then Achilles does not start out in this opening scene to provoke a quarrel with Agamemnon; his purpose, rather, reflecting his concern for the troubled situation in which the army is in, and which his commander has ignored, is to invite Agamemnon's participation in an action that might save the army from disaster.

Agamemnon is enraged when Chalkas announces that it is his refusal to return Chryses's daughter to her father that has caused the plague of deaths besetting the Achaian army. He explodes in anger at the priest and demands from the army an immediate replacement for the prize he is now willing, he says, to give up for its sake. Men have been dying day after day and Agamemnon's concern is only with the *immediate* replenishing of his soon-to-be-

Understanding the Iliad

diminished supply of prizes—something that can be accomplished only by depriving one of the other heroes of an honor, since the army has no collection of undistributed rewards at its disposal. Now it is Achilles's turn to feel outrage, and he expresses it by denouncing Agamemnon's "greed," but his annoyance is still restrained as he offers Agamemnon the opportunity make up his losses three and four times over when the Achaian army takes Troy.

Agamemnon's greed, however, and his pride in status cannot be satisfied by a promise of future reparation, but must be fed by tangible compensation here and now, so Agamemnon warns that if the army does not voluntarily award him a suitable prize, he will strip one of his important commanders, Achilles, Ajax, or Odysseus, of a prize for his own benefit. Achilles has been disciplined and moderate in his dealings with Agamemnon up to this point, but this is a provocation that he cannot endure. Agamemnon's manifestation of greed and self-aggrandizing abuse of authority against the background of ongoing deaths that afflict the Achaian army is most certainly not a heroic code value and merits no respect. Achilles is now unrestrained in his denunciation of Agamemnon's mercenary orientation and ingratitude toward those who have come to fight for his cause. His contempt is so great for his commander that he announces that he will abandon the expedition against Troy and return home to Phthia. It is Agamemnon's arrogance and folly that then escalates the quarrel to a much greater level of intensity. He responds with outrage to Achilles's threat to withdraw from the coalition of Achaian forces and sarcastically invites him to "flee" if his spirit drives him to that course of action. Then, Agamemnon, as punishment for Achilles's "insubordination" and as a sign of how little regard he has for him, declares that he will go to Achilles's hut and replace the prize he now will give up, the daughter of the priest Chryses, with Achilles's own prize. At that time, he says, "you will see just how much/Better I am than you, and another will fear/To equate himself to me and to liken himself to me face to face" (1.186-87). It is at this point that Achilles comes close to total loss of self-control:

> ...Grief descended on Achilles and in his shaggy
> breast his heart pondered two choices: whether
> he should draw his sharp sword from his thigh and

43

Leon Golden

> Break up the assembly and slay Agamemnon, or
> subdue his wrath and check his temper. (1.188-192)

We know that Achilles does not take the next step and kill Agamemnon, and more than one level of motivation is at play here. Athena appears on the scene and advises Achilles that it will be in his best interest not to proceed with the slaying of Agamemnon. His own human intelligence, symbolized by Athena, would easily recognize that the killing of Agamemnon would terminate the expedition in failure and send it retreating homeward without achieving the rewards of glory and wealth that had been its goal. Thus we have here an example of the "double motivation" on divine and human levels I discussed in the last chapter. A third motivation for keeping Agamemnon alive at this point is, of course, the narrative requirements of the poem, which makes it necessary for Agamemnon to be present at later stages of the story both to illuminate the scope and depth of Achilles's wrath and to provide the mechanism for Achilles's return to war after the death of Patroclus.

In his negotiations with Agamemnon in book 1, Achilles has so far moved through the following stages: (1) a respectful request that a prophet be consulted on how to terminate the disaster afflicting the Achaian army; (2) a promise to offer full protection to that prophet no matter what cause or guilty party he identifies; (3a) a denunciation of Agamemnon's greed when he demands an immediate replacement of the girl the priest says he must return to her father if the disaster afflicting the army is to end; (3b) a moderation of his just-expressed contempt for Agamemnon by the suggestion that he is welcome to take three or four times the value of the girl when the Achaians capture Troy; (4a) the intensification of his anger to the point of heightened condemnation of Agamemnon's greed and arrogance when he refuses to defer to a future date the replacement of the prize he is going to lose and threatens to substitute for her the prize of one of his generals; (4b) his mounting anger and exasperation with Agamemnon leading to the announcement of his withdrawal from the expedition against Troy and intention to return home; (5) his readiness to kill Agamemnon after his commander announces that he will take Achilles's prize, Briseis, as a substitute for the daughter of Chryses he will now return to her father; (6) finally, his savagely escalating

Understanding the Iliad

verbal assault on Agamemnon which substitutes for the physical violence he has just been contemplating:

> "...Agamemnon, saturated with wine, With a dog's
> eyes and a deer's heart! You've never dared in
> your heart to arm for war with the host nor to go
> on an ambush with the best of the Achaians. That
> seems to you to be death. Far better it is for you
> to take away prizes throughout the wide camp
> of the Achaians if someone opposes you. You
> are a people devouring king, since You rule over
> worthless men. Otherwise, son of Atreus, This
> would be your last act of insolence....
>
> And this will be my great oath to you: Truly desire
> for Achilles will come one day upon all the sons
> of the Achaians; at that time you will not be able,
> although grieved, to help them, when many fall
> dead at the hands of man-slaying Hector. But you
> will mangle the heart within you because you did
> Not honor the best of the Achaians." (1.225-44)

At this point, while Briseis still remains in Achilles's hut as his prize, the situation is not yet irreparable. Achilles, excessively provoked, has not said anything much more extreme than the prayer Chryses offered to Apollo when the plea for the return of his daughter was harshly rejected:

> "Hear me, god of the Silverbow, who protects
> Chryse, and Cilla, and rules mightily over Tenedos,
> the Sminthian God who wards off plagues! If ever
> I have roofed over a temple that pleased you Or
> burned fat thigh pieces of bulls and goats for you
> Accomplish for me this prayer: Let the Danaans pay
> for my tears through your arrows!" (1.37-42)

The lethal violence unleashed by this prayer was quelled by Agamemnon's reluctant submission to the god's will, but the fearful consequences of Achilles's oath are not stanched by any human agency until a heavy price in unnecessary suffering and

Leon Golden

death has been paid. Nestor attempts to mediate the quarrel by emphasizing to Agamemnon that it was the army who bestowed the prize on Achilles and so he should not interfere with that award; and to Achilles he recommends restraint before someone whose status is superior to his own. Nestor's efforts fail in regard to Agamemnon because his excessive concern for rank and status will brook nothing that even remotely and irrationally suggests insubordination (he says of Achilles "he wishes to rule everyone and to be king over everyone and to give commands to everyone" (1.288-89); and Nestor fails in Achilles's case because the injury inflicted on him is a deeply penetrating assault on his dignity and value as a human being resulting from Agamemnon's treatment of him as if he were a coward and despicable human being. It will not be too long, but it will be too late, when Agamemnon comes to realize how disastrous his actions have been. Earlier, he had yielded to Apollo's priest and saved the army from disaster. Now he has no perception how traumatic his provocative humiliation and alienation is going to be of his best general and his indispensable field commander.

The dispute between Agamemnon and Achilles is not carried out on a level playing field. Agamemnon's grievance is framed in terms of a perceived act of insubordination by a lower-ranking officer, a fracturing of military discipline; Achilles, however, has sustained insults ("coward," "worthless human being") the effect of which has been to degrade and dehumanize him. Later, when Agamemnon determines that it is necessary to reverse the actions that resulted in Achilles's alienation from the army, it is a relatively easy task for him to maintain military discipline and protect his role as commanding general by using his authority to attempt to *reward* with many prizes the subordinate whom he had *disciplined* earlier by stripping him of one prize. Agamemnon never comes to understand the magnitude of the error he has committed in his treatment of Achilles and is only saved, eventually, from the consequences of his folly by the death of Patroclus in battle. Now, however, he compounds the serious misdemeanor of insulting and belittling Achilles with the felony of carrying through his threat and stripping him of his prize. From this point on, there will be no return, no healing of wounds, no moderating of suffering, until great disasters have struck the Achaian army and awakened Agamemnon to his earlier folly. He will learn the hard and bitter lesson that a perceived challenge to one's status and rank is far

Understanding the Iliad

from being equivalent to the abuse of someone else's human dignity. After suffering the humiliating loss of Briseis, Achilles pleads with his mother, Thetis, to approach Zeus and:

> "To see if he may be willing to help the Trojans and
> to hem the Achaians in around their sterns and
> the sea, while they are being slain, so that all may
> profit From their king and the son of Atreus, wide
> ruling Agamemnon may recognize his madness
> because he did not honor the best of all the fighting
> Achaeans." (1.408-12)

With the return of his daughter to him, Chryses's anger has no further reason for existence and he prays to Apollo to fulfill his prayer and ward off now this unseemly plague from the Danaans. When Achilles loses his prize, he has no occasion to rescind his curse on the Achaian army until the death of Patroclus changes the murderous focus of his wrath. Instead, we learn that he kept on raging beside his swift-faring ships, nor did he keep going to the assembly where men win glory, nor ever to war, but he kept eating his heart out, remaining in place and kept desiring the cry of war and war itself. There will be escalating defeat and much suffering before Agamemnon's intransigence buckles; and before there can be any resolution for Achilles of his troubled state, his *anger* will have become *blind rage,* a distinction of immense importance, as we shall see, in psychoanalytical terms.

Our next major focus on Achilles will come in book 9, but we should not ignore information we get from references to him in the books intervening between 1 and 9 and from comparisons we can make between Achilles and other major characters who appear in those books. In book 2, lines 377-80, Agamemnon admits that he started the quarrel over a girl with Achilles and recognizes that Troy's fate would have already been sealed if he and Achilles were in agreement with each other. But that recognition does not move Agamemnon to any action. In book 3, the emphasis is on Paris, not Achilles, but certain significant differences and similarities between the two should be brought to mind by events in this book. Paris's flight from Menelaus in hand-to-hand combat of course offers a major contrast between the two. We will never see Achilles fleeing in fear from any adversary. Yet both Paris and Achilles share a willingness, for different reasons, to violate

Leon Golden

the heart of the orthodox heroic code by refusing opportunities for "killing and being killed" that other warriors would normally find obligatory. Paris makes the individualistic decision to avoid war and death when they conflict with his hedonistic impulses; and Achilles makes the individualistic decision to absent himself from heroic code activity, and even solicits the defeat of his own army by divine intervention, when emotional and psychic pain caused by his commander's insults provokes him to elevate, like Paris, a dominating personal interest over any commitment to the larger community of which he is a part. Contrasting the behavior of Paris and Achilles leads us to reflect on an important insight about Achilles's character in the poem. Some of our most striking impressions of Paris are at those times when, yielding to the hedonistic impulse, he pursues and savors pleasure. In book 3, he responds to Helen's sarcastic rebuke of his cowardly reluctance to face Menelaus in hand-to-hand combat as follows:

> "Don't rebuke my spirit, Helen, with harsh words.
> For now Menelaus defeated me with the help of
> Athena, another time I'll defeat him for there are
> also gods on our side. But come now, let us turn
> to making love. For never has desire so enfolded
> my heart, not when I first took you from lovely
> Lacedaemon and sailed with you in my swift faring
> ships and made love to you on the island of Cranae,
> as I desire you now and sweet desire seizes me."
> He spoke and led the way to the bed and Helen
> followed. (3.438-47)

Later, in book 11, Homer offers us the following description of the superficial wound Paris inflicts on Diomedes:

> ...Paris drew the bow's centerpiece back, and
> struck—for not in Vain did the arrow fly from his
> hand—the flat of Diomedes's right Foot; and the
> arrow passed clean through and was fixed in the
> Ground. And Paris laughing merrily leaped from
> his hiding place And boasted: "You've been hit and
> my arrow didn't escape my hand in vain. I wish I
> had struck deep into your belly, killing you. So the

Understanding the Iliad

Trojans might recover from their pain..." (11.375-382)

As we reflect on these scenes in which Paris makes something of a game out of war, it is easy to become aware how totally absent from Achilles's experience throughout the poem are pleasure and laughter. We recall the words that describe his animosity against Agamemnon in book 1:

> ...Grief descended on Achilles and in his shaggy breast his heart pondered two choices: whether he should draw his sharp sword from his thigh, and Break up the assembly and slay Agamemnon or subdue his wrath and check his temper? (1.188-192)

From this time on, pain, suffering, and grief will shadow his life. Tracking Achilles's role in the *Iliad*, as we are now doing, means tracing the unfolding of his emotional and psychological anguish until epiphany leads to transformation, although not to pleasure in any sense that Paris would understand, in the final two books of the poem. We learn much about the character of Achilles by comparing the unfolding of his experiences of pain and sorrow in the *Iliad* with the hedonism of Paris, the rich pleasures Hector enjoys within his family, and, especially, through the depiction of the eloquent series of joyful scenes on the "Shield of Achilles" in book 18. All of these evocations of pleasure and human happiness provide a gloomy emphasis on the contrasting melancholy of Achilles's life. We will need later to review in detail the essentially cheerful and positive message of the shield and its ironic positioning as a weapon of savage destruction in the hands of a hero driven berserk by massive grief.

Through book 19 of the poem, the relationship between Achilles and Agamemnon is a bitterly destructive one. We will better understand the issues which divide them if we focus on Agamemnon's rather different interactions with some of his other commanders. In book 4, we have an instructive opportunity to make such a comparison. Here, Agamemnon ranges through the Achaian army, stirring them up for combat with the Trojan forces. He has occasion to rebuke Menestheus and Odysseus for holding back from the attack. His words are harsh:

49

Leon Golden

> "Son of Peteus—a king nurtured by Zeus—And
> you, excelling in evil devices, crafty, Why do you
> stand apart, cowering, and wait for others? It is
> most fitting for the two of you to stand In the front
> ranks and take part in blazing battle; For both of
> you are first to hear of a feast I am giving Whenever
> we Achaians prepare a banquet for the elders.
> Then it pleases you to eat roast meat And drink
> cups of honey-sweet wine as long as you wish;
> But now you'd look on gladly to see ten columns
> of Achaians Fighting in front of you with pitiless
> bronze." (4.338-48)

Odysseus's response is equally harsh as he defends his courage in battle and calls Agamemnon's words as empty as the wind. When Agamemnon notes Odysseus's anger, his reaction is quite different from the harsh insults he hurled at Achilles in book 1:

> "Zeus-born son of Laertes,
> Odysseus, with many wiles,
> I don't berate you excessively or exhort you;
> For I know the spirit in your breast knows kindly
> Counsels. Your thoughts are also mine. But come
> now,
> We will make amends later if any harsh word has
> been said
> And may the gods make all this vanish from us.
> (4.358-63)

Next Agamemnon encounters Diomedes and Sthenelus standing by their horses, not yet in action:

> Lord Agamemnon saw Diomedes and rebuked him
> Addressing him with winged words:
> "O son of fierce Tydeus, tamer of horses, why are
> you
> Cowering? And why do gaze anxiously at the
> bridges of war?
> Tydeus did not behave like this." (4.368-72)

Understanding the Iliad

Sthenelus responds with anger at Agamemnon's taunts, just as Odysseus did, but Diomedes remonstrates with Sthenelus and adopts a different tone:

> With a grim look from beneath his brows mighty Diomedes
> Said "Be silent, my friend, and follow my advice.
> I don't resent it that Agamemnon, the shepherd of the people
> Is urging the well-greaved Achaians to fight;
> Great glory will come to him, if the Achaians slay the
> Trojans and capture holy Ilion. And great grief will come
> To him if the Achaians are slain. But come now let both of us be mindful of furious battle." (4.411-18)

The differences in these encounters between Agamemnon and other officers and his quarrel with Achilles are large and informative. We recall that in the face of Agamemnon's failure to act against the disaster striking the Achaian army, Achilles called an assembly, recommended— respectfully—that a priest be invited to explain what needed to be done to alleviate the catastrophe, and promised—at the request of the priest—to provide him with complete protection no matter who or what he identified as the cause of the problem. None of this was done in any defiant or provocative way toward Agamemnon, but in the spirit of bringing about a resolution to a serious problem. It was when the priest identified Agamemnon as the party responsible for the plague that Agamemnon announced that he had no intention of having a prize removed from him without replacing it, even at the expense of one of his subordinate officers. Then it was that Achilles denounced him for greed and a failure of leadership. This, in Agamemnon's mind, was intolerable insubordination and he struck back against Achilles with dehumanizing insults, suggesting that he go ahead and flee, a coward and worthless human being, whose absence from the army would mean nothing to him.

The conditions setting off the bitter exchange between Agamemnon and Achilles which provoked charges of greed and worthless military leadership, on the one hand, and generated

Leon Golden

dehumanizing allegations of cowardice, on the other, are not repeated in the encounters between Agamemnon and Odysseus and Diomedes. Agamemnon does not call either Odysseus or Diomedes a coward, but is engaged in fulfilling his leadership responsibilities by exhorting two of his best commanders to exhibit their highest level of combat effectiveness. One of them, Odysseus, resents the implications of Agamemnon's exhortations and receives an apology because no insubordination was involved; the other, Diomedes, recognizes the right of the commander-in-chief to sharpen the fighting edge of his subordinate commanders and accepts the rebuke without rancor. In these cases, Agamemnon's actions were within the rules and custom of military practice; tough and effective generals and officers of every rank have acted similarly in all wars. For the most part there is the expectation that military discipline requires that lower-ranking officers and soldiers accept the exhortation and rebuke of their commanders in the same spirit as Diomedes. Agamemnon's taunting aspersions against Achilles were insults calculated to injure deeply—not a strategy aimed at exhorting troops to the highest level of desire and effectiveness in combat:

> "Flee, then, if your heart urges you to, I am not going to
> Beg you to stay on account of me. By my side are others
> Who will honor me, and especially Zeus the lord of Counsel.
> To me, you are the most hateful of the Zeus-nurtured kings
> For always strife and wars and battles are dear to you.
> If indeed you are strong, a god, I believe, gave that to you.
> So go home with your ships and rule the Myrmidons.
> I take no account of you nor do I have any concern for
> Your explosions of anger...." (1.173-81)

In other wars, officers who have behaved like this have been "fragged"—killed by their own men who grew to hate and

Understanding the Iliad

disrespect them—which is precisely what Achilles was on the verge of doing to Agamemnon.[9] Agamemnon knows that implying that Achilles is a coward is an outright lie which, as is his intention, will cause pain to the recipient of the insult. Only he has no idea how deeply that slur will penetrate and traumatize the sensitive layers of Achilles's psyche and create a disaster of overwhelming magnitude for the Achaian forces. Agamemnon has made the mistake of treating Achilles as someone like Odysseus or Diomedes who will either make a controlled, if angry, response to insults or pass over them as permissible under the rules of military custom. He has no idea how vulnerable and unprotected Achilles's psyche is—a factor of essential importance in determining the future direction of the action of the poem and one to which I will give close attention as this study proceeds—and so he has no idea of the murderous instincts he has unleashed in the best soldier and field commander in his army.

The despair and pain which Achilles experiences in the poem up to the death of Patroclus are a direct result of the emotional and psychological trauma he has sustained from Agamemnon's insult and the willingness of the army to tolerate Agamemnon's actions against him. We will learn a great deal more about this in book 9. While justifiably emphasizing the psychological pain of Achilles, we should also note subtle foreshadowings by Homer of the way in which Achilles will ultimately transcend his afflictions. I noted in the last chapter that the *Iliad* depicts several impressive moments when the course of war is interrupted and the demands of the orthodox heroic code are abrogated by the unexpected appearance of a lifesaving truce or act of compassion between adversaries. The first of these involves Diomedes and Glaucus in book 6, who discover that they have a guest-friend relationship dating back to their grandfathers that permits them to call a truce between themselves that transcends the "kill and be killed" mandate of the orthodox heroic code. I noted that another such truce occurred in book 7, when heralds on both sides interrupted what could have been a fight to the death between Hector and Ajax. We should view these events as thematic preparations, foreshadowings of the most important truce of all in the poem, the cessation of hostilities for eleven days, requested by Priam and generously granted by Achilles, so that the burial of Hector can take place with full honors. If we are to comprehend the meaning of the *Iliad* fully, we must carefully assess the reason why Homer

Leon Golden

has brought his great epic, encompassing so much of war along the way, to its eloquent climax in a scene of pacification and tranquility that focuses on honoring the vanquished warrior and not exalting the triumphant victor.

Hector is the central figure in book 6 and there are certain differences between him and Achilles that are most informative in regard to an understanding of Achilles's character. In this book, Hector returns to the city he is defending to get his mother, the other women, and the elders to pray for divine help for the Trojan forces in the war. We see him as a disciplined soldier who will not accept an offer of wine from his mother because it might reduce his strength, nor an invitation from Helen to rest for a while from the toil of war because he knows his place is with his army as its commander, a role he plays also when he chastises and provokes Paris to leave his dalliance with Helen return to the serious business of war. We see him in the role of husband and father in a scene of rich, familial emotion when Andromache comes running to greet him on his visit home from the battlefield:

> She then met him and the nurse came with her
> Holding their tender child to her breast, only a baby,
> The dear son of Hector, like a beautiful star,
> Whom Hector used to call Scamandrius
> But everyone else Astyanax;
> For only Hector guarded Ilion.
> He looked at his son and smiled silently;
> Andromache stood close to him, shedding tears,
> And clasped his hand... (6.399-406)

Andromache pleads with him not to go back to the deadly fighting on the battlefield where he is likely to leave her a widow and their son an orphan. Instead, she urges him to fight close to the city, where he can protect it and his family at the same time. He listens sympathetically to Andromache's pleas but his response is the message of the orthodox heroic code:

> "My wife, all of this is a concern to me but
> Very much do I feel shame before the Trojans and
> their wives,
> With their trailing robes if I should,
> Like a coward, shun my part in war; nor does

Understanding the Iliad

My spirit desire it since I have learned to be brave
And always fight in the front ranks of the Trojans,
Winning great glory for my father and myself."
(6.441-46)

He expresses concern for his family but even more for his city, for which his duty, pride, and sense of honor require of him a willingness to sacrifice his life. Then:

...glorious Hector reached for his son but back into
The bosom of his well-girdled nurse the child
swerved,
Screaming, terrified of his father's appearance
Frightened of the bronze and the horsehair crest he
Perceived waving fearfully from the top of the
helmet.
At this his father and revered mother laughed;
And glorious Hector quickly removed the helmet
from his head
And placed it gleaming on the ground.
Then he kissed his dear son and tossed him in his
arms
And said a prayer to Zeus and the rest of the gods:
"Zeus and all the gods: grant that this son of mine
Become, as I am, distinguished among Trojans,
Courageous in his strength, and ruling Ilion with
might.
And one day someone might say that he is far
better than his father
When he returns home from war; and may he bring
bloody spoils,
Having killed a foe. And may his mother rejoice."
(6.466-481)

When comparing Achilles and Paris, I noted that despair and sorrow are salient characteristics of Achilles's life, in contrast to Paris's untroubled pursuit of pleasure. When comparing Achilles and Hector, we observe how *isolated* Achilles is from the sustaining human relationships which enrich Hector's life. Both his mother, Hecuba, and Helen are eager to comfort Hector and give him support but it is, of course, his wife, Andromache, who

Leon Golden

expresses the deepest emotional bond with him. She fears for his life and also for the consequences of his death for herself and their son. No one in the *Iliad*, even those closest to him on the human level, expresses this kind of deep affection for Achilles or sorrow for the death that is to come for him, and on the divine level, Thetis's exchanges with him are anthropomorphically and rather routinely maternal. She knows that he is destined for an early death, and she commiserates with him about his fate, but as she eagerly promises to seek the favor of new armor for him from Hephaestus, we do not sense the agony which Andromache makes known to us for the dangers Hector faces. Overwhelmed by sorrowful emotion, Andromache attempts to prevent Hector from returning to the open battlefield, but Thetis becomes an ally of Achilles in his return to the fighting and killing of Hector that she knows will seal his death, saying:

> "Yes, my child. This is truly not a bad thing to defend your Comrades brought low in face of utter destruction. (18.128-29)

Homer does not find the occasion to put into words the affection he suggests exists between Achilles and Briseis, the prize Agamemnon strips from Achilles, when she goes "unwillingly" with his heralds, Talthybius and Eurybates, to become the possession of a new master. Achilles's conversations with Patroclus, his single, close human contact in the poem, focus on the military situation and the vengeance he is pursuing against Agamemnon, and are devoid of intense personal references. It is only between Priam and Achilles that Homer depicts a relationship of great emotional depth based, in the end, on a common experience of enormous suffering that leads to mutual respect, affection, and sympathy; but this is quite different from the strongly affirmative bonds that unite Andromache and Hector in familial love. The tenderness that exists between Hector and his son—beautiful as a star—does not reflect any experience Achilles knows of, except that when he clasps the wrist of Priam so as to take away his fear at the end of his tormented journey in the poem from wrath to compassion, he displays an emotional response not unlike Hector's paternal love for his son. For the most part, however, Achilles appears before us lonely, isolated, and separated from the warmth of human contact that we observed in

Understanding the Iliad

Hector's case. Murderous rage and alienation from the embrace of enriching human relationships characterize him throughout the poem from his near-killing of Agamemnon in book 1 to the berserk orgy of slaughtering Trojans in books 20-22. Only in books 23 and 24 does he escape the emotional and psychological nightmare of separation from the human community from which he has bitterly exiled himself. What the precise source is of Achilles's rage, joyless isolation, and bitter and unrelenting addiction to brutal, punishing revenge, and how and why those emotions are transformed into a series of impressively compassionate acts in the final two books of the poem—that, I suggest, is the dominant theme of the *Iliad* which we must pursue.

Book 9 is a storehouse of information about Achilles's character and emotional and psychological state. At the beginning of the book, Agamemnon is in one of his despairing moods and urges the army to return home and give up the project of taking Troy as a lost cause. Diomedes opposes this suggestion of accepting failure in their enterprise and the army strongly supports him against Agamemnon, who then summons a council of elders. There Nestor points out the obvious—that Achilles's abandonment of the army as a consequence of the humiliation he suffered at Agamemnon's hands is the cause of their great distress. With his officers adamantly opposed to retreat, and Nestor's evaluation of the cause of their dilemma clearly accurate, Agamemnon is forced to admit to the folly, the madness of his abusive treatment of his most powerful warrior. Agamemnon, who is far from having penetrating psychological insight, interprets the animosity generated by the argument in book 1 exclusively as a matter of a prize of honor given and rescinded. His remedy, then, given the dire circumstances in which the army finds itself, is to overcome the misfired disciplinary action against Achilles by bestowing a long list of such rich and impressive prizes on him as to stir wonder and amazement in Achilles's peers. In addition he promises to return Briseis herself, untouched, whose removal from Achilles had precipitated the disastrous quarrel, and to offer him the choice of one of his own three daughters as his bride without having to pay a bride price for her. Nestor sums up the positive view of the offer Agamemnon is now making to Achilles when he says "Most glorious son of Atreus, Agamemnon, lord of men, the gifts you offer lord Achilles are no more to be despised" (9.163-64).

Leon Golden

Unfortunately, Nestor and the other Achaian commanders are as blinded to the real source of Achilles's wrath, as is Agamemnon.

Nestor then recommends that Agamemnon send Phoenix, Ajax, and Odysseus, accompanied by heralds, as emissaries to Achilles to present the offer of Agamemnon's extensive treasure of gifts and to plead with him to return to battle and save the Achaian army from disaster. Nestor's intuition as to who should be chosen as ambassadors is an excellent one, for when they came to the camp of the Myrmidons and found Achilles playing the lyre and singing of deeds of glory, his words of welcome are warm indeed as he addresses them as "the Achaians dearest to me even in my wrath" (9.198). After Achilles offers his visitors a generous and worthy feast, Odysseus begins the serious business of their mission. He describes the desperate situation of the Achaian army and pleads with Achilles as follows:

> ....But up then if you wish even at this late moment,
> To save the sons of the Achaians brought low by
> the din of war
> Among the Trojans. You, yourself, will feel grief
> hereafter
> Nor is it Possible to find a cure once evil has been
> done;
> But far sooner think how you will turn aside
> The day of doom from your countrymen.
> My friend surely to you Peleus commanded
> On the day when he sent you to Agamemnon from
> Phthia:
> "My son, Hera and Athena will give you strength
> If they wish, but you must restrain the proud spirit
> In your breast. A friendly spirit is
> Is better. Leave off from strife, the contriver of evil
> So that Argives, young and old, will honor you
> more." (9.247-58)

Odysseus has made it clear that the Achaians are in desperate straits ("this is the last chance to save your countrymen") and reminds him of a flaw in his character that his father, Peleus, had warned him about, the need to "control your proud spirit." Then he focuses on the gifts of atonement which Agamemnon is ready to bestow on him as a worthy incentive to abandon his anger.

Understanding the Iliad

Odysseus repeats the long and impressive list of those gifts so that we cannot miss the extraordinary measures Agamemnon has taken to overcome the ill will generated by the quarrel in book 1. If Achilles should think that Agamemnon's change of heart is not enough to justify the abandonment of his wrath, Odysseus has other, very important incentives to offer:

> "But if the son of Atreus is excessively hateful
> To your heart, himself, and his gifts, pity
> All the other Achaians in distress throughout the
> army,
> Who will honor you like a god for truly you would
> win
> Great honor from them. For now you might kill
> Hector as he would approach very close in
> Possessed by a destructive rage. Since he says
> That there is not any one equal to him of the
> Danaans
> Whom the ships brought here." (9.300-06)

Odysseus has enumerated all of the powerful incentives that he expects should overcome the wrath of Achilles: there is the desperate need for survival of his allies including the three ambassadors who have to come to him and he has greeted as "the Greeks I love best;" there is the acknowledgement of enormous error by Agamemnon symbolized by the impressive caliber of gifts he is ready to bestow on Achilles; independently of Agamemnon, there is the gratitude and honor Achilles will receive from the entire army which—in his absence from the battlefield—is beset by hopelessness; and, finally, there is the highest of all heroic code prizes, the chance to attain glory that will endure forever by defeating the greatest of the Trojan warriors.

The shocking fact is that none of this means anything to Achilles. The possibility of the imminent destruction of the Achaian army and even of "the Greeks I love best," the attempted atonement of Agamemnon for his abusive treatment of Achilles by the lavish gifts he now offers, and the opportunity for killing Hector—the highest level of heroic code achievement possible in the Trojan War—are declared by Achilles to be impotent, totally worthless inducements for him to abandon the scorching wrath

Leon Golden

engendered by the traumatic humiliation he suffered at the hands of Agamemnon in book 1.

Achilles's response to the pleas made by the ambassadors who are his best friends in the Achaian army is uncontrollably emotional. He declares that he does not have any further desire to fight Hector, but will return home to Phthia the next day, and invites his close friends to come down to the sea and watch him, their one and only hope for survival, disappear from their midst. The pleasure he takes in announcing his planned withdrawal from Troy completely—the cruelly provocative proposal to them to witness his departure—shows cold insensitivity to the feelings of those who have been his friends, and in Phoenix's case, much more than his friend, in the past. He announces, in addition, that Agamemnon's vast store of offered gifts are of no interest to him:

> "Hateful to me are his gifts. I honor them at a hair's worth.
> Not even if he gave me ten or twenty times
> As much as he now possesses and other things besides
> Not so much as comes to Orchomenus or so much as comes
> To Thebes in Egypt where the greatest number
> Of possessions are stored up in the houses,
> Thebes with its hundred gates, and two hundred men
> With their horses and chariots go forth through each of them.
> Not if he gave me gifts as many as the grains
> Of sand or dust would Agamemnon persuade
> My heart until he had paid me back
> For all the outrage that stings my heart.
> I will not marry the daughter of Agamemnon,
> Son of Atreus, not though she rivaled
> In beauty golden Aphrodite and in weaving
> Was a match for gleaming-eyed Athena." (9.378-90)

This is a response that develops out of intense emotional pain that is in desperate search of relief and finds it only by applying with extreme destructiveness the *lex talionis,* the law of revenge, the law of an eye for an eye and a tooth for a tooth. Achilles

Understanding the Iliad

even goes so far as to denounce and abrogate the authority of the orthodox heroic code that declares that the achievement of enduring glory through the risking of one's life in the courageous act of killing or being killed represents the highest level of human achievement. He states emphatically:

> "For not to me is it worth my life, not so much as
> they say the
> Well-inhabited city of Troy possessed previously, in
> the time of
> Peace before the sons of the Achaians came, nor
> so much as the
> Marble threshold of the Archer, Phoebus Apollo,
> encloses in rocky
> Pytho. For cattle and goodly sheep can be pillaged,
> tripods and
> Chestnut horses can be acquired; but that the life of
> a man
> Return again neither pillaging nor seizing avails
> once it
> Has passed the boundary of his teeth." (9.401-09)

He then refers to the two fates his mother, Thetis, said were available to him: death with enduring glory if he remains to fight at Troy, or a long life without glory if he abandons Troy and returns home. He says he is ready to choose the inglorious second alternative for himself and advises others to do the same. This is a complete reversal of the ethic by which, we must assume, he has lived his life up to now and which so dominates the perspective of the warriors in the *Iliad*. This is not Achilles's real belief and ultimately we know that Achilles will not act on it, but it is an uncontrollable expression of his tormented emotional state that has provoked an insatiable appetite for revenge for the pain he has suffered and has swept from his mind the nobler aspirations and commitments of the past. In his response to Achilles, Phoenix reminds him of their close relationship, of how he became a foster father to the very young Achilles, of how Peleus sent him with Achilles on the expedition to Troy when he was still too young to know anything of assemblies and war and how it was Phoenix, at Peleus's behest, who taught Achilles to be skilled in speaking and brave in deeds. Phoenix has known Achilles for a very long time

Leon Golden

and in a relationship resembling very closely that of father and son, but even he has no perception of the dark cloud of anguished resentment that hovers over his much-suffering spirit.

It is Agamemnon's offer of gifts that Phoenix believes makes all the difference now. He tells Achilles that no matter how badly the Achaian army needed him, he would never ask him to return to their aid if Agamemnon had not bestowed a lavish store of gifts upon him. He reminds him of the story of Meleager, who did not respond at first to offers of rewards to defend his city but later, too much later, did fight and defeat the enemy. He received however, Phoenix emphasizes, no prizes for his services. Phoenix urges him not to lose the rewards Agamemnon is offering, for his honor will be less that way, even if he eventually does return to war on the side of the Achaians. Achilles sharply retorts to Phoenix that he does not need or want that kind of honor, and then very firmly instructs him to hate Agamemnon simply and only because of his hate for him.

The long, loving, and nearly paternal relationship which had existed between Phoenix and Achilles does not stand in the way of Achilles threatening to sever that tie if Phoenix does not make an absolute commitment to loathe Agamemnon in the same way that Achilles loathes him. *You cannot be his friend and mine also* is the harsh mandate he lays upon the tearful old man who is attempting to save the Achaian army from disaster, while at the same time honoring Achilles; but Achilles's mind is totally occupied with his own personal psychological and emotional pain inflicted by Agamemnon in book 1, and he is unable and unwilling to summon from within himself any sympathetic sensitivity for the deep anguish of another human being, no matter how close his relationship with that person has been. Ajax detects that the iron will of Achilles will not be changed or softened and bitterly speaks of him as savage, cruel, hard-hearted and filled with malice without regard for the respect and honor his friends have shown him more than anyone else in the entire army. He reminds him that even a murderer can pay compensation and reenter society and, if that is the case, he finds it utterly incomprehensible that Achilles would not accept in the place of one single girl taken from him seven magnificent women as compensation and many other gifts. He begs him to replace his cruel insensitivity to those who have come to express their love, respect, and need for him with comparable generosity and respect on his part. All this is in vain.

Understanding the Iliad

In spite of Ajax's pleas, Achilles's wrath rises again to threatening heights as he tells the embassy to report back to Agamemnon a new message, the cruelest of all—he will do nothing to help the army until Hector, "killing Greeks as he goes and torching the fleet" approaches Achilles's camp and then, and only then, after his friends and allies have fallen victim to the carnage of war, will he step forward to confront and defeat Hector. Here he shows once more total insensitivity to the needs and emotional pain of those he claims to love the most in the Achaian army. Agamemnon and the other Greek commanders are stunned by the report brought back by the embassy, and the final evaluation of Achilles in book 9 is Diomedes's regret that Agamemnon had offered the gifts and his denunciation of Achilles's arrogance.

Book 9 is critical for understanding the *Iliad* because we penetrate much more deeply into the driving force of wrath in the character of the central figure of the epic. In book 1, the death of Agamemnon was the principal focus of Achilles's attention before he decided against that action; now he imagines and savors the death of the entire Achaian army, with the exception of his own troops. In book 1, feeling betrayed by the lack of support of the army's leaders in his quarrel with Agamemnon, he felt justified in abandoning them with a warning that they will eventually pay the price for their commander's mistakes; but now, with the hand of friendship extended to him by those he loves best in the army, he scorns and rejects their support and willingly, cruelly, arrogantly rejoices in his isolation from the army that needs him so badly and he exults in the power he has to consign that army to total destruction. Jasper Griffin accurately describes Achilles's response to Odysseus and the other ambassadors as "the most splendid speech in Homer, in range and power" a speech that:[10]

> ...is an explosion of hoarded anger, which floods out with pathos, irony, bitterness, and the passionate rejection of the life and death of a hero if it must be lived on terms without *charis*, gratitude and honor due to a man who accepts the heroic destiny and performs it.

Griffin also correctly identifies Achilles's speech as "the high point" of book 9 as it displays "the emotional nature, the depth of hurt and anger, which drives Achilles into a position which neither

Leon Golden

he nor anyone else in the poem wholly understands."[11] The force pressing Achilles to his extreme position is, as Griffin remarks, one that readers have found difficult to comprehend and forgive. Owen comments that "the cause of his wrath may seem to us trifling and out of all proportion to its intensity as absurd almost, as the cause of Lear's wrath with Cordelia."[12] Edwards believes that the view taken of the motives for Achilles's decision to abandon the Achaian army to its grim fate is "crucial for the interpretation of the *Iliad* as a whole and the tragedy of Achilles." On this point, he is certainly correct. He is also correct to call attention to the quandary so many have felt concerning the motives for Achilles's unrelenting, indeed, escalating wrath:[13]

> All thoughtful readers of the poem will form their own opinions about why the hero acts as he does, and whether he is acting rightly or wrongly, and those opinions may well change with rereading and reconsideration. It is characteristic of a supreme and "classic" work of art that no single interpretation is likely to satisfy generally or for long, and every society, every individual, every experience of the work will be, and should be, different. Every reader brings to a work his or her own presuppositions, preferences, and philosophy, just as every actor will interpret a role in a great drama differently...

Edwards then offers a summary of the very different ways Achilles in this very critical book 9 of the poem can and has been interpreted by readers:[14]

> Achilles may be viewed in this book as the supreme hero whose ideals rise above those of his peers and who challenges the accepted norm of the society in which he lives; as a spoiled and sulky child who is holding out for more coaxing than he has yet received; as a victim of *Atê*, blind folly, who makes a decision that must bring disaster for himself and others; as the incarnation of *hubris*, the arrogance that almost automatically brings retribution and ruin; as the model of Aristotle's conception of the hero destroyed by some

Understanding the Iliad

hamartia, or his picture of the *megalopsuchos*, the great-souled man who must demand the full measure of honor from his associates.

Since all of these judgments are possible under the conditions that have so far obtained for interpreting the *Iliad*, we are faced with the unsatisfactory prospect of having to accept a series of mutually contradictory verdicts concerning the impulses provoking Achilles's actions. Resolving the question of Achilles's motives on the basis of the individual tastes and preferences of the members of an audience, as Edwards suggests, is a conceivable approach, but it means that we accept the thesis that Homer has not precisely defined and communicated his intentions to us, and has constructed his epic in a way that allows for the maximum ambiguity of interpretation. That, of course, is a possibility, but one to which we should resort in the case of the *Iliad*, or any great work of art, only when *all* other possibilities are exhausted. Edwards, to his credit, does not leave the problem at that level of inconclusiveness. He takes the very reasonable position that "if the *Iliad* is intended to be a whole in the form in which we have it, Achilles must reject the supplications [of Agamemnon's embassy] at this point [book 9]" for the unfolding narrative strategy of the poem requires that Achilles not return to the war until after the death of Patroclus at the end of book 16. Thus the poet, Edwards says quite correctly, "must therefore find reasons for Achilles to refuse to return in Book 9" and he offers the following approach, within the narrative structure of the poem as we have it, to establishing a cogent explanation for Achilles's action in rejecting the appeal of the envoys.[15]

> The question then becomes, not "Why does Achilles reject the envoys in Book 9?" but "Has the poet produced reasons consistent with the characterization and plot? Are they connected with events and situations that come before and after? Is the motivation of significant interest as an aspect of general human reasoning or emotion, as a credible reaction to a recognizable situation in human society?"

Leon Golden

As I see it, Edwards's mandate intelligently requires us to demonstrate that the destructive wrath so inexplicable to others, which Achilles exhibits in book 9 is (1) consistent with his developing characterization throughout the work and the process by which the plot of the poem progresses from beginning to the middle to the end in a necessary and probable manner and, more importantly, (2) demonstrates a credible response, psychologically, emotionally, and intellectually to conditions we recognize as rooted in the reality of the human condition.

For Edwards and many other readers, the primary focus for understanding the source and nature of Achilles's wrath is in his inflamed relationship with Agamemnon and he offers an analysis of this relationship with which, in the main, most readers would have no difficulty in agreeing. There is no doubt, as Edwards points out, concerning the intense dislike Achilles has for Agamemnon on the basis of the abusive treatment he received from him in book 1, and there is no doubt that the gifts which Agamemnon offers are insufficient compensation in his mind for the contempt with which he was treated at that time. As Edwards states, "it is the humiliation of Agamemnon that Achilles desires" and not the receipt of lavish gifts that would bring honor to Agamemnon for his generosity and emphasize Achilles's subordinate status to the commander who could bestow such gifts.

Wrath directed at Agamemnon by Achilles, no matter how filled with hate and violence it might be, could be understood as falling at some extreme point within the normal range of human emotion. I assert that Achilles's wrath, however, falls so far outside that normal range of human experience that it requires an explanation far different from the one Edwards and other critics have offered. If we are to understand the character of Achilles fully in the critical events of book 9, and in the entirety of the *Iliad*, then the issue that must be resolved is not why he hates Agamemnon so much and wants to punish him severely, but *why he cannot restrain himself from spreading the disastrous effects of that hatred over so many others, close friends and innocent bystanders, in the Acaian army*. Edwards justifies Achilles's attitude by saying that "Achilles' decision to go home, when he feels that he has been deserted by his friends is thus the only possible one."[16] Now, while it is true that the army did not rise in full rebellion against Agamemnon over the redistribution of a prize in book 1 (an act that does not seem to have had for them the same cosmic magnitude it did for Achilles),

Understanding the Iliad

it is most certainly not true that the army has deserted Achilles in book 9. Their relationship to him at this point is the very opposite of desertion, as the three representatives of Agamemnon declare their need, respect, and love for him. It is Achilles's willingness to ignite a savage conflagration of destruction that will sweep over the entire Achaian army that is the crucial issue at this point in the *Iliad* as it is the overwhelmingly important characteristic that defines who Achilles is, has been, and will become in the poem.

The *Iliad* proceeds on its fatal course to the death of Patroclus, to the death of Hector, and to the deaths of many Trojans and Achaians because Achilles's wrath is *irrational and unbridled* in the scope of its application, its toleration of the massive victimization of friend and foe alike, and its total dedication to the *lex talionis,* the law of revenge, without guidance or discipline from the civilized conscience to which, repeatedly in book 9, his closest and dearest friends appeal. We will follow the theme of Achilles's wrath through scenes of massacre on the battlefield and the desecration of Hector's body in books 20-22; but we will complete our investigation of that theme only in books 23 and 24, when Achilles's ongoing evolution as a human being leads him to transcendentally ennobling acts of kindness and compassion that extinguish the force of irrational wrath in the poem. In summary, it is Edwards's position that Achilles refuses to return to the army in book 9 because:[17]

> (1) when envoys come to him in this book, they come not because of their sympathy with him or in revolt against Agamemnon, but as the obedient spokesmen for his hated antagonist;
> (2) he does not want gifts of Agamemnon's giving, gifts that would honor his enemy as much as himself;
> (3) he feels that he has been deserted by his friends and thus the decision to go home is the only possible one.

As countervailing evidence to this view, I would like to cite the following excerpts from the conversation between Achilles and the three envoys in book 9:

Achilles

67

Leon Golden

"Welcome, truly friends have come—there surely
Must be great need—you who are the dearest of
the Achaians to me, even in my wrath." (9.197-98)

Odysseus
"But if the son of Atreus is excessively hateful
To your heart himself and his gifts, pity
All the other Achaians in distress throughout the
army, Who will honor you like a god, for truly you
would win Great glory from them." (9.300-3)

Phoenix
"Thus I have suffered much and labored much for
you Because I knew that the gods would not
Make me the father of my own child.
But I made you my child, god-like Achilles,
So you would ward off unseemly ruin from me
But, Achilles, tame your proud spirit. It is not
Necessary for you to have a pitiless heart.
Even the gods themselves, are flexible
Although in them there is greater excellence, honor
And strength. And yet men, in supplication, turn
them Aside with sacrifices and kindly prayers and
libations And the savor of burnt offerings whenever
someone transgresses and errs." (9.492-501)

Ajax
"...But Achilles
Has made his proud spirit savage in his breast,
Merciless, as he is, nor does he take account
Of the friendship of his comrades with which we
Honored him exceptionally above all others by the
ships.
He is pitiless.
...But in your breast gods have placed
A spirit that is implacable and evil
Because of one girl; but now
We offer you seven by far the best
And many other gifts besides. Make your heart kind
And respect the house of which you are the master.
We have come under your roof from the host of the

Understanding the Iliad

Danaans and we yearn beyond all others to be nearest
and dearest to you among the Achaians, however many
they may be." (9.628-32, 636l-42)

Whatever Achilles may have felt about the army in book 1, there is nothing in tone or content here that suggests that he harbors a contemptuous feeling for the three envoys as "the obedient spokesmen for his hated antagonist"—just the opposite—in the space of two lines, he greets them as "friends" (*philoi*) and as those who are "dearest" (*philtatoi*) to him even in his anger. I emphasize again that in coming to an understanding of Achilles's decision to abandon the Achaian army in book 9, a decision which both Edwards and I agree is critical to an interpretation of Achilles's character and of the epic as a whole, *it is his cruelly insensitive treatment of the three men he describes as "dearest" to him,* not his animosity toward Agamemnon (for which there is a clear and ample explanation) that is of the greatest importance and demands a convincing explanation that I do not believe has yet been forthcoming. Odysseus's speech (passage 2) addresses Edwards's second point, that by accepting gifts from Agamemnon, Achilles would bestow honor on the giver as well as the receiver of those gifts. Odysseus is aware of reasons why Achilles would refuse gifts from Agamemnon and offers him an honorable, meaningful, altruistic alternative: He says that if Agamemnon and his gifts are detested by him, he should think of all those who suffer the brunt of the war who will bestow great glory on him. As Edwards maintains, Achilles does not need or want gifts from Agamemnon, and now Odysseus has given him a cogent and lofty reason for refusing the gifts and returning to the war on behalf of those who are his "dearest" friends and many others who face annihilation because of his absence. All that Achilles needs to comply with this request is compassion and sensitivity to the pain of others, but those are precisely the humane feelings that he does not possess at this time and will not come to possess until after the death of Patroclus sets in motion Achilles's berserk massacre of Trojans at the Skamander River and the slaying and savage mutilation of Hector's body which unfold in books 20-22. Then the gradual suppression of Achilles's wrath takes place in the funeral games of book 23 and reaches its

69

Leon Golden

climax in the transforming experience of his encounter with Priam in book 24. Achilles's lack of compassion and his insensitivity to the pain and sorrow of his closest friends and many others in the Achaian army receives even greater emphasis in the speeches of Phoenix and Ajax (passages 3 and 4). Phoenix has been a foster father, a teacher and guide to Achilles in his developing years. Of the three envoys, he has the closest bond with Achilles. Yet when he pleads for Achilles to save the Achaian army from destruction, we recall that Achilles curtly tells him not to irritate him with his pleas for reconciliation with Agamemnon, and his sharp warning that he cannot maintain friendship with Agamemnon and still retain Achilles's friendship. While Achilles acknowledges that Phoenix is like a second father to him, he is ready to sever his close ties with him if he is not willing to obey his command to hate Agamemnon and he is completely unwilling to give any credibility to the pleas on behalf of the entire Achaian army of the man who guided and protected him through childhood and youth. Finally, it is Ajax who repeats the supplications of Odysseus and Phoenix that Achilles be merciful to those who depend upon him, and tame his pitiless heart, since even murderers can subdue the hearts of the relatives of the murdered man by paying compensation, and can then go on living again in their own country. In a literal translation of 9.641-42 Ajax says "we desire especially among as many of the other Achaians as there are to be nearest to you and dearest to you." These statements of love and loyalty to Achilles are *not* rejected by Achilles. He tells Ajax that:

> "All your words appear to accord with my own thoughts. But my heart swells with rage when I recall those things By which the son of Atreus degraded me among the Argives As if I were some despised vagrant. (9.645-48)

What we see here is Achilles standing before us in book 9 privileging his adamant hatred of Agamemnon (one that he will not have any difficulty in abandoning after the death of Patroclus) over his concern for those who, on their arrival, he greets as his friends and recognizes as the ones who are dearest of all the Achaians to him. It bears repeating that whatever may have happened in book 1, the embassy does not approach Achilles here as unsympathetic agents of Agamemnon—quite the contrary—they eagerly and

Understanding the Iliad

intensely seek to unite with him in the common cause against the Trojans, which was the original goal of the expedition they have all made together. It is Achilles who has deserted from that cause to pursue his private vendetta against Agamemnon in preference to the common good of the army as a whole. Moreover, Achilles does not denounce the embassy, in Edwards's words, as "the obedient spokesmen of his hated antagonist" but offers them a warm and friendly welcome and, in the end, even agrees with Ajax's description of his cruel and unfeeling behavior by responding to him that everything he says seems to be in accord with his own thoughts. Hainsworth's comments on Achilles's replies to Ajax and Phoenix in book 9 are pertinent and perceptive in seeing the similarity of the responses in both cases:[18]

> Akhilleus's reply to Aias is couched in simple terms but conveys a terrible sense of resolve and continuing outrage. Aias said in effect "I never thought you would treat your friends like this in your own house," and Akhilleus has no reply to that devastating comment....Thus in spite of his provocative language Aias is treated in a comradely manner which stands in contrast with Akhilleus' treatment of Phoenix. His response is the same in both cases, admitting the force of the argument but citing his feelings toward Agamemnon as an insuperable bar to action. Phoenix is treated to the imperative mood and a sharp reminder of his duty towards his patrons; the address to Aias follows [a] conciliatory pattern.

Hainsworth is clearly right that the stinging blow to his psyche delivered by Agamemnon makes Achilles unable to abandon a rage that will have a murderous effect on his own friends and allies, and prevents him from responding to pleas for humane compassion from them. Those friends have given him cogent reasons for coming to their aid, but he fills the universe with his own pain, his own sorrow and, for him, nothing else matters. Why his personal anguish becomes such an inhumanely destructive force that dominates the action of the poem until the end of book 22 is the question we must answer if we are truly to understand Achilles and comprehend the central theme of the *Iliad*.

Leon Golden

We have seen that the orthodox resources of literary criticism have not given us a definitive answer to this question but have, rather, allowed for a multiplicity of diverse and conflicting views concerning the possible motivations of Achilles. One point, however, that is quite clear about Achilles is that he is torn apart by the powerful emotion of uncontrollable rage. Now rage is a phenomenon very much under the scrutiny of students of human psychology and it is thus to relevant insights from the psychoanalytical community that I would like to turn now in an attempt to fathom as deeply as possible the origin and nature of Achilles's wrath as it courses through books 1, 9, and through what Bernd Seidensticker has aptly called Achilles's "bloody butchery (*blutige Metzelei*)" at the Scamander River in books 20-22. The use of scientific analysis for defining features of Achilles's character and personality will enable us to understand much better the penetrating insight of Homer's intuitive poetic genius. I offer, first, these remarks by the psychiatrist, Alexander Lowen, on narcissistic rage:[19]

> The emotion correlated with fear is anger. But narcissists are as incapable of expressing or feeling anger as they are of any other feeling. It is true that narcissists can and do at times fly into a rage. Indeed, one can say that a tendency to fits of rage is characteristic of this disturbance. Isn't rage the same as anger? Although there is a strong element of anger in an outburst of rage, the two expressions are not identical. Rage has an irrational quality—just think of the phrase "a blind rage." Anger, in contrast, is a focused reaction; it is directed toward removing a force that is acting against the person....Rage, however, it not in line with the provocation; it is excessive. Nor does rage subside with the removal of the provocation; it continues until it is spent. And rage is destructive rather than constructive. Indeed, rage is tinged with a murderous intent.... It is significant that an outburst of narcissistic rage be closely tied to the experience of frustration, of not being able to get one's way; in other words, of feeling powerless.... Why is this reaction called narcissistic rage?

Understanding the Iliad

> Recognizing the murderous quality to all such
> reactions, we can postulate that the insult provoking
> the reaction must strike a vital cord.... Describing
> the rage as narcissistic tells us that the insult was to
> the person's sense of self, that it was a narcissistic
> injury. The experience was one of humiliation,
> of being powerless. As we have seen, it is this
> experience of humiliation that underlies narcissists'
> striving for power. Through power they believe they
> can wipe out the insult.

It is clear that Lowen's discussion correlates with much of
Achilles's behavior. It is rage, of course, murderous rage which
Achilles feels when he is just seconds away from drawing his
sword and killing Agamemnon in book 1, when he beseeches his
mother, Thetis, to plead with Zeus to bring death and destruction
on the Achaian army as appropriate punishment for Agamemnon's
insulting humiliation of him and, of course, when he immerses
himself in the savage killing spree, we will discuss in detail, that
follows upon Patroclus's death and reaches its climax in the brutal
mutilation of Hector's corpse. His request to Thetis to intercede
with Zeus on his behalf expresses the deadly character of his rage
very clearly:

> "...see if he may be willing to help the Trojans
> And to hem the Achaians in around their sterns
> And the sea, while they are being slain, so that all
> may profit
> From their king and the son of Atreus,
> Wide-ruling Agamemnon,
> May recognize his madness because he did not
> honor
> The best of all the fighting Achaeans." (1.408-12)

To atone for the insult he has sustained, he wants Achaian
soldiers to die in abundance in order to teach Agamemnon and
the Achaian army a truly harsh lesson that is fully justifiable in his
mind, but in no one else's. Achilles bitterly awaits the slaughter of
Achaian troops so that the army can feel the pain of Agamemnon's
flawed leadership. We should note here that on a principle related
of that of "double motivation," the principle that allows for the

Leon Golden

causation of the same action to occur on both the divine and human levels, Achilles's abandonment of the Achaian army has the same destructive effect on that army as the direct intervention of Zeus would have had.

Lowen tells us that rage "is not in line with the provocation; it is excessive." Achilles says that not even if Agamemnon offered gifts as numerous as grains of sand or dust would he soften the fierce hatred he feels. The pleas of the three men he loves the best in the Achaian army who have come as an embassy from Agamemnon to him do not divert him from the extreme punishment he proposes to inflict on the Achaian army. He agrees with Ajax's assessment of the inhumane harshness of his stance, but responds to him that, although he agrees with his words, he nevertheless is filled with rage when he thinks of the insults and humiliation to which Agamemnon has subjected him. Achilles's mind will not be changed, he says, until Agamemnon has fully repaid the pain he has suffered. What has Agamemnon done to Achilles? Taking away his prize is merely the external cover for something far more sinister. Agamemnon has delivered a crippling blow to Achilles's essential dignity, his sense of self, and provoked from him an outburst of rage—narcissistic, murderous rage. Lowen tells us that "describing the rage as narcissistic tells us the insult was to the person's sense of self, that it was a narcissistic injury. The experience was one of humiliation, of being powerless." Achilles makes it clear that he was humiliated by Agamemnon, that he was treated like a worthless human being and a coward. And once Achilles decides in book 1 (for narrative and thematic reasons) that he cannot kill Agamemnon on the spot, then he is not only humiliated but is powerless to remove or repay the insult except by the consequences of a murderous rage that neither the offer of lavish prizes nor the expressions of need, respect, and affection of those he loves the best in the Achaian army will be able to overcome. Lowen tells us "it is this experience of humiliation that underlies narcissists' striving for power. Through power, they believe that they can wipe out the insult." The power that Achilles seeks is to make Agamemnon, and the entire army, as powerless and disgraced, or more so, as he himself was in book 1.

"...And this will be my great oath to you:

Understanding the Iliad

> Truly desire for Achilles will come one day upon all
> the sons
> Of the Achaians; at that time you will not be able,
> although
> Grieved, to help them, when many fall dead at the
> hands of
> Man-slaying Hector. But you will mangle the heart
> within you
> Because you did not honor the best of the
> Achaians." (1.238-244)

Lowen tells us that rage does not "subside with removal of the provocation; it continues until it is spent. And rage is destructive rather than constructive. Indeed, rage is tinged with murderous intent." Achilles says that not until he is repaid fully for the pain he has suffered will his rage at Agamemnon end; and the murderous intent of this statement is clear, since there is no other mechanism for achieving this repayment than retaliatory humiliation inflicted on Agamemnon, at a huge cost of the lives of friends and foes alike. We recall that Achilles has said the Achaians will appreciate Agamemnon's flawed leadership when soldiers fall dead in battle. In book 11, Achilles savors the possibility of his retaliation as he watches wounded Achaian soldiers being taken out of the battle and summons Patroclus to go to Nestor and identify the casualties. He says to Patroclus, "now I think that the Achaians will be standing about my knees, begging me, for an intolerable necessity has come upon them" (11.609-10). Achilles rejoices to see the wounded in the Achaian army, for that is the only way he can conceive of by which the narcissistic injury that has been inflicted upon him will be remedied. Hainsworth touches on narcissistic aspects of Achilles's speech here when he says:[20]

> ...we should not see therefore in Akhilleus' curiosity
> [about the identities of the wounded Achaians] the
> first stirrings of some concern for the effects of his
> anger on his friends. On the contrary the opening
> verses of the speech sound a distinctly vindictive
> note, and it is appropriate that they should; the
> more Akhilleus is perceived as concerned solely
> with his own honour, the greater will be felt the

Leon Golden

shock of remorse at the disaster to Patroklos which
that selfish concern brings about.

Patroclus does go on a mission to Nestor and learns of the
dire straits in which the Achaian army now finds itself. His report
to Achilles comes at the beginning of book 16 where, weeping with
sorrow for the Achaian suffering he has witnessed, he is pitied by
Achilles, who still shows no sign of remorse for being the agent
of that suffering. He sarcastically inquires of Patroclus what the
cause of his tears may be. Is it bad news from back home—the
deaths of one of their fathers, perhaps? Then he gets to the real
point:

> "Or do you grieve for the Argives, how they perish
> By the hollow ships on account of their
> transgressions?
> Speak and don't hide it in your mind..." (16.17-19)

To which Patroclus replies:

> "Achilles, son of Peleus, best by far of the Achaians,
> Don't feel such outrage; so great is the distress that
> has Overwhelmed all of our men, so many who
> Were once our best; they lie among the ships
> struck and wounded." (16.21-24)

Achilles is still very much under the influence of the pain
inflicted on him by Agamemnon's insults in book 1 when he
responds to Patroclus with his reasons for allowing the Achaian
army to suffer. "Terrible grief," he says, "comes upon my spirit
and heart/when someone more powerful wishes to rob one who
is his equal and take away his prize," (16.52-4) and he angrily
repeats the insult, "dishonored vagrant," that Agamemnon had
hurled at him. A little later, he adds that the Trojans "soon in their
flight would fill the mountain-streams with their corpses if Lord
Agamemnon had showed me kindness" (16.73-75). It is clear that
the narcissistic injury he suffered in book 1 torments him greatly.
He, however, agrees to the suggestion Nestor made in book 11
that Patroclus be permitted to wear Achilles's armor and lead the
Myrmidons into combat in order to reverse the tide of battle. Then
he gives the following directions to Patroclus:

Understanding the Iliad

"But obey me so that I may put
In your mind the sum of my advice
So that you may win for me great honor and glory
From all the Danaans and they send back that most
beautiful girl and, in addition, offer splendid gifts.
When you have driven them from the ships,
Come back, even if the loud-thundering husband
of Hera Grants you the winning of glory, nor should
you desire to wage war against the Trojans who
love war apart from me. You will diminish my honor."
(16.83-90)

The climax of his address to Patroclus is most significant:

"I pray to father Zeus and Athena and Apollo That
not one of the Trojans might escape death, As
many as they are, nor any of the Argives, But that
the two of us would survive In order that we, alone,
might tear down Troy's Sacred battlements." (16.97-
100)

Achilles's speech is replete with evocations of the narcissistic
injuries he has suffered. He rejoices that Greeks lie dying and
wounded on the battlefield because of their transgressions, a
reference to the army's unwillingness to rebel against Agamemnon
for his treatment of Achilles in book 1. He expresses again the
pain he feels at being stripped of his prize and being treated like
some dishonored vagrant. He asserts that the Trojans would now
be routed and suffering disaster if only Agamemnon knew how to
respect him. His instructions to Patroclus are, as Hainsworth said,
motivated by selfishness to a large degree although with some
thought about Patroclus's ultimate safety. He wants Patroclus to
win *him* honor and then to withdraw from the battle so as not to
detract from the ultimate glory of defeating the Trojans that he
wants to reserve for himself. In spite of his rage at the insult he
sustained in book 1 at Agamemnon's hands and the absence of
intervention by the army to redress his grievance, he has relaxed
his intransigence toward the Achaian army up to the point that
their ships not be burned and the army stranded on the beaches
of Troy. Since he had earlier pronounced himself ready to sail

Leon Golden

home on his own and leave the rest of the army to Hector's destructive power, we must speculate on what has changed his attitude here. He has explicitly told Patroclus that he does not want him to defeat the Trojan army, because that would diminish his honor. If Patroclus is successful, however, it would also strip him of the power to make Agamemnon pay a heavy penalty for his abusive actions in book 1. It would not be possible for Achilles to humiliate Agamemnon, a retaliatory goal that was clearly on his mind when he rejected the overtures of the envoys in book 9, if Patroclus, and not he, himself, were responsible for the defeat of Hector, for if Patroclus handed the Achaian army a decisive victory over the Trojan forces, Agamemnon would be free of any necessity to supplicate Achilles for the assistance needed to save his army. With the help of Lowen's analysis, we previously linked Achilles's behavior in books 1 and 9 to the oppressive sense of powerlessness to punish Agamemnon directly that provokes murderous rage in the narcissistic personality. Sending Patroclus into the battle to *forestall* a Trojan victory but not yet to *enable* an Achaian victory preserves for Achilles, when the circumstances are right, the power of retaliatory punishment against Agamemnon, the power of making Agamemnon suffer the same kind of painful humiliation that he inflicted on Achilles in book 1.

We have seen that Achilles concludes his mandate to Patroclus with a prayer to the mighty forces of Zeus, Athena, and Apollo. He asks the great deities of the cosmos to strip the world bare of every Greek and Trojan fighting at Troy so that only he and Patroclus would be left alive to take Troy by and for themselves. This icy supplication illuminates the grandiose, insensitive, totally unrealistic and thus ultimately unstable core of Achilles's narcissistic rage. We see his grandiosity and lack of feeling in his willingness to punish with extreme severity *anyone* who stands in his way or attempts to block his will whether they be a demonstrated enemy like Agamemnon or close friends like Odysseus, Phoenix, and Ajax. He declares that, other than Patroclus, he has no need of anyone else in the world and he has such an exaggerated view of his own empowerment and such a lack of sympathy for other human beings that he can envision with equanimity the total destruction of whole armies.

Achilles is the greatest of all warriors on the Trojan battlefield, but entertaining a vision of such immense grandiosity and such total insensitivity to other human beings that he can pray for the

Understanding the Iliad

disappearance from the face of the earth of Trojans and Achaians alike, is not heroism but a dangerous psychological flaw. We know, of course, that it is not Homer's plan to end his great epic with Achilles reveling in murderous, narcissistic rage. The wrath of Achilles triggered in book 1, inflamed in book 9, slightly moderated but basically unchecked in book 16, and then, transferred from its original target that has now faded into insignificance to an object of all-consuming hatred, explodes, as we have noted, into the berserk fury of battlefield slaughter that culminates in the desecration of Hector's corpse in book 22. In all of these scenes, Achilles is a still unperfected, developing human being who is under the influence of character flaws that have been noted earlier in the poem. We recall that in book 9 Odysseus reminds Achilles that his father, Peleus, sent him off to war with the words:

> "My son, Hera and Athena will give you strength If they wish, but you must restrain the proud spirit In your breast. A friendly spirit is better. Leave off from strife, the contriver of evil so that Greeks young and old will honor you." (9.2541-58)

In book 11, Nestor reminds Patroclus that when he and Achilles were on the point of going to war:

> "....Old Peleus instructed his son, Achilles, always to be the best, distinguished above all, but he commanded you Menoetius, son of Actor, thus: 'My child, Achilles is higher than you in birth but you are older, though in strength he is very much superior. But speak well wise words to him, and advise him and point the way for him and it will be to his advantage to obey.'" (11.783-89)

Before the action of the war at Troy began, Peleus had warned Achilles about the dangers inherent in his "proud spirit" and he had encouraged Patroclus to provide needed guidance for his son still struggling toward maturity. Achilles's uncontrolled "proud spirit," which was a source of anguish for Peleus, continues however to shape his behavior all the way through to the mutilation of Hector's corpse in book 22. Remember Diomedes's words in book 9 when

Leon Golden

the returning envoys report Achilles's rejection of Agamemnon's offer of reconciliation:

> "Most noble son of Atreus, king of men,
> Agamemnon, You should have never have begged
> his excellency, Achilles, Offering him countless
> gifts; Even without that he is a man of arrogance."
> (9.697-99)

Up to the end of book 22, Achilles, as the possessor of an unyielding proud spirit, as the fierce and unbending administrator of a destructive and indiscriminate vengeance, as one who will not blunt his rage at the earnest solicitations of those he loves best in the Achaian army, is far from demonstrating qualities necessary for heroic status. Even if one wanted to give him full credit for his military prowess, Homer allows him to demonstrate his impressive capability in that regard in only three of the twenty-four books in the poem, and those episodes are *not* the climax of the poem but only the furious prelude to the crowning point of the *Iliad* that we reach in the final two books of the poem and, in their mood of humane compassion, clash radically with the atmosphere of the battle scenes. We are under obligation to seek a persuasive thematic connection between the actions of Achilles savagely in pursuit of vengeance in books 1-22 and the sympathetic and compassionate Achilles in books 23 and 24. If we do not make that connection, then we face an option that has been unacceptable to the best Homeric scholars: to deny to the *Iliad* unity as a work of art. This problem disappears, however, if we view the *Iliad* as an account of a hero who undergoes change and development within the poem, one who reaches full maturity through experiencing a life-enhancing epiphany derived from an agonizing encounter with the nature and meaning of human suffering. Thus, it is only after the impressive transformation of Achilles takes place in the final two books of the poem that we are able to put all of the pieces together from book 1 onward, so as to see the whole plan of Homer's epic with its focus on an evolving and evolved Achilles as the central hero of the *Iliad*. The goal of establishing the unity of the *Iliad* in the way I have suggested lies ahead of us. Before that, we must return to Achilles in the crisis he faces after the death of Patroclus and take note of the preparatory steps to his reentry into the war, the pregnant symbolism of the shield Hephaestus

Understanding the Iliad

fashions for him to replace the armor lost to Hector, his escalating rage against Hector and the Trojans, and the berserk orgy of slaughter through which he survives the loss of Patroclus in books 20-22.

In our earlier discussion, we have seen how isolated Achilles is from affirmative human relationships and the pleasures that flow from them when compared with Hector. In book 16, he expresses no need for the sustaining support of family or community, such as the one surrounding the great Trojan prince; only one loyal subordinate suffices to make his grandiose ambitions against the outside world effective. Up to now, without allies to support him, Achilles has had the power to control all of the situations in which he has found himself. Had he been willing to kill Agamemnon in book 1, he could have exercised ultimate control over his commanding general, but the consequences—as we have seen—were unacceptable and he settled for another strategy he had full power to enforce—ruthless revenge that would bring the Achaian army and Agamemnon to their knees by abandoning his allies and withdrawing completely from the war. I have spoken of the psychoanalytical interest in the kind of murderous rage which Achilles exhibits; there is a similar interest from this quarter in the kind of reckless, grandiose, and insensitive application of punitive and retaliatory power which also characterizes Achilles. Lowen comments on some dangerous aspects of the phenomenon of power as follows:[21]

> In many ways, power is a denial of one's humanity. As we have seen, through power the narcissist attempts to transcend feelings of helplessness and dependency. But isn't a certain helplessness a part of the human condition? We don't ask to be born, in general, and we have no say over when we will die. We cannot choose with whom to fall in love. There are many instances in which we are not masters of our fate. Yet our helplessness in these areas is tolerable because all human beings are in the same boat. And we need each other to counter the darkness, to keep out the cold, to provide meaning to existence. Human beings are social creatures. It is with other people that we find the warmth, the excitement, and the challenge of life. And only

Leon Golden

> within the human community do we dare face the
> frightening unknown. Narcissists are not exceptions
> to this human need. They, too, need people. But
> they dare not acknowledge this need. To do so
> is to admit and face their vulnerability.....But even
> if the psychopathic personality [one of the more
> advanced manifestations of narcissism] doesn't
> acquire a flock of followers, he or she must have at
> least one devotee, whether a lover or prostitute. In
> other words psychopathic personalities must have
> someone who needs them. They cannot be alone.
> And the relationship must be one in which they
> have control.

After book 16, Achilles must face the fact that for the first time
in the poem, he is now totally powerless to change or reverse a
circumstance hostile to himself, the calamity that has befallen
him in the death of Patroclus. If we apply Lowen's analysis to
Achilles, we see that the facade of invulnerability has been ripped
away from the presence he has heretofore shown the world as he
recognizes a dark and debilitating impotence to control forces that
affect him adversely. He is also, for the first time, in the disastrous
condition that Lowen describes of being completely alone. When
Antilochus brings Achilles news of Patroclus's death at the
beginning of book 18, we see Achilles as we have never seen him
before:

> ...A black cloud of grief descended on Achilles.
> In both his hands he took black dust
> And poured it over his head, disfiguring
> His handsome face. Black dust settled on
> His scented cloak as his great body lay
> outstretched
> In the dust, and with his own hands he tore
> And mangled His hair.... Antilochus wailed and wept
> And held Achilles' hands and his noble heart
> Groaned for he feared he would cut his throat
> With his knife. (18.22-27, 32-34)

If this epic is, at its core, a *Bildungsroman* as I envision it to
be, a story of personal evolution, development, and maturation

Understanding the Iliad

on Achilles's part, then it is at this point that he faces the greatest crisis of his life. Patroclus had supplied the thin reed of human support that was all that Achilles needed, psychologically, to sustain the dangerous forces, characteristic of the grandiosity and insensitivity to human suffering that his unique physical power allows him to exhibit with impunity, a type of behavior which the psychoanalyst describes as narcissistic. Now Achilles stands at a crossroads: Can he accommodate himself to the reality of the insurmountable limitations of power that define the human condition which he has now, for the first time, desperately confronted? Can he fill the void of absent human connections left by Patroclus's death, shed the façade of invulnerability by which he has operated for so long and which psychoanalysts tell us is a sham, as if we did not know that on our own, and negotiate sustaining human relationships that nurture rather than betray his inner self? Suicide is an immediate option, but Antilochus prevents him from exercising that option, an outcome that Homer will not allow because it is his intention to lead us to a climactic vision of Achilles triumphant in his perfected humanity, not Achilles destroyed by a corroding narcissism.

In Homer's narrative, Thetis then comes to Achilles in his troubled state and asks:

> "My child, why are you crying? What grief
> has come upon your heart? Speak, don't hide it.
> Those things have been accomplished by Zeus for
> which you prayed earlier in supplication that all the
> sons of the Achaians be hemmed in at the sterns
> of their ships and suffer terribly In need of you."
> (18.73-77)

Through the ferocity of his untamed wrath, Achilles has achieved what had been his greatest desire, *revenge* against Agamemnon and the Achaian army, but that revenge is cold comfort to him now as he explains his mood and his plans to Thetis:

> "My Mother, the Olympian has accomplished this
> for me, But what pleasure is there for me since my
> comrade has perished, Patroclus, whom I honored
> above all others, as equal to myself. I have sent

Leon Golden

> him to his death. And his armor Hector has stripped
> From him when he killed him, armor that was
> huge and beautiful, A marvel to behold, that the
> gods gave to Peleus as a Magnificent gift..." "...But
> now may I win noble glory, And force someone of
> the Trojan women and deep-breasted Dardanian
> women to wipe away the tears From her tender
> cheeks, and to groan loudly." Let them know that all
> too long I have stayed my hand from war." (18.79-
> 81, 121-25)

On a principle related to that of "double motivation," and by analogy to the discussion Achilles had with Athena when he was on the verge of slaying Agamemnon in book 1, this conversation with Thetis could very well be understood as a psychologically *realistic* reflection within his own mind as to what the effect of his wrath has been, and what his future actions must be. In his conflict with Agamemnon, Achilles's inflamed appetite for revenge has exacted an immense penalty in battlefield casualties from his enemy as he follows and exceeds the mandate of the ancient *lex talionis,* "an eye for an eye and a tooth for a tooth." The consequence of achieving his intensely desired vengeance has, however, been to suffer, himself, a searing personal calamity that has brought him to the brink of suicide without in any way altering his addiction to devastating retribution as the means for subduing the world outside of himself to his will. He savors the vision of a Dardanian wife or mother sobbing and groaning because of the death of a loved one at his hands. The vengeance against the Achaian army has been cruelly punitive but Achilles will pursue a far more ferocious retaliation against the killer of Patroclus and his Trojan forces. We will be viewing the next, escalating phase of his quest for revenge as we follow his actions through book 22. This is, however, the appropriate time, at the transition point between vengeance taken against the Achaian army and the impassioned revenge to be inflicted on Hector and the Trojan forces, to consider how Achilles's unflinching performance as an agent of the *lex talionis* affects our evaluation of him as a potential epic hero. The impulse for vengeance plays such a dominant role in the motivation of Achilles's behavior from book 1 through book 22, that there is a chance that some might think of it as part of his heroic *persona,* especially for readers who, as has sometimes happened

Understanding the Iliad

in the past, find books 23 and 24 unnecessary and unrelated to what they feel is the real story of the *Iliad*, the war that is unfolding on the Trojan battlefield. If, however, we view the *Iliad* in the precise form Homer has bequeathed it to us, and as a unified story depicting the emotional and psychological evolution of Achilles as a human being, then we must give books 23 and 24 a special place of importance in any valid interpretation of the epic.

What then can we say about the dominating force of revenge in Achilles's behavior and his status as a hero? We gain support again from the psychoanalytical community if we reject the idea that the vengeance inspired humiliation of Agamemnon at such high cost in Achaian casualties, the unnecessarily brutal massacre of foes at the Scamander River also driven by revenge, and the punitive, conscienceless mutilation of the corpse of Hector are manifestations of heroism. The psychiatrist James Masterson has written that the goal of the therapeutic process is to assist the patient toward "the mastery of the talionic principle—that deepest and most ancient of human impulses to exact revenge by taking pleasure in inflicting on others the hurt that one has experienced and that "a person's objective sense of the rightness and wrongness of human conduct is an achievement, an end product of a long, slow tedious process which requires... the mastery of the talionic impulse...[22]

Psychiatrist Thomas J. Brady remarks:[23]

> It seems to me that the value we put on revenge, based on some twisted notion of fairness and reciprocity, is astonishingly destructive, represents the worst rather than the best of human nature...
>
> I was once told, and I have passed the assertion on to my patients and even friends, that one cannot be called truly civilized until he or she has tamed the talionic impulse, that is the compulsion to enact the *lex talionis,* let the punishment fit the crime, an eye for an eye and so forth. It is the law of revenge, which we sometimes confuse with justice, and creates around us a sort of jungle mentality, the opposite of civil society.

Leon Golden

From the perspective of the psychoanalytical community, the mastery of the talionic impulse, the compulsion for revenge, is a prerequisite for traversing the rites of passage to the highest level of civilized maturity. Ultimately, Achilles will achieve this impressively humane status at what is, in my view, the thematic climax of the *Iliad*. Before that happens, however, his submission to the talionic impulse will reach new heights of unpitying violence. In book 18, in a subtle and eloquent way, I believe that Homer causes us to reflect deeply on the dehumanizing characteristics of vengeance, the talionic impulse, that has played such an important role in Achilles's behavior up to this point and that will govern his activities through the end of book 22. The poet accomplishes this by means of a strategy similar to one he used in book 14, where he placed the hedonistic escapade with comic overtones involving Hera's seduction of Zeus directly in the midst of scenes of human suffering in grim and deadly encounters in war to which Zeus and Hera have made themselves coolly indifferent. In book 18, Homer separates the first phase of Achilles's murderous wrath aimed at Agamemnon from the second phase of his mounting rage and unbridled urge for revenge against Hector with an elaborate description of the shield which Hephaestus has fashioned for him. The powerfully suggestive iconography of the shield brings to the fore affirmative human experiences which directly contradict in mood and tone the volatile emotions of the talionic impulse, which is the motivating force within Achilles until the end of book 22.

Oliver Taplin, acknowledging a large debt to Schadewaldt, Reinhardt, and Marg, has offered a very perceptive analysis of the role the shield plays in the *Iliad*.[24] "Why is the shield of Achilles," Taplin asks in the first sentence of his article, "instrument of war in a poem of war, covered with scenes of delightful peace, of agriculture, festival, song, and dance?" It is a most important question and Taplin and I will give both shared and different answers to it because of our overlapping and yet somewhat different perspectives on what the central theme of the *Iliad* is. For Taplin, the shield, along with many similes and certain key scenes in the poem, communicates to us Homer's balanced assessment of the positive and negative characteristics of war, a view that denies validity to the position of those who see the *Iliad* as advocating the simplistic ethic of winning glory by "killing or being killed." My previous analysis of the heroic code theme in the poem shows that I am in full agreement with Taplin on this

Understanding the Iliad

point, but I have argued that the central theme of the poem is not war, *per se,* but the changing and evolving character of Achilles, in relation to which war is very often a background and, for a short period of time, the twenty-seventh day of the *Iliad* during which books 20, 21, and 22 take place, the stage on which his pursuit of vengeance achieves maximum force before it undergoes a significant transformation.

From my perspective, the answer to Taplin's question must include the issue of war and peace but go beyond it and sharply focus on Homer's presentation of Achilles to us as a character who undergoes dynamic changes between the climactic expression of his impulse for revenge, the talionic impulse, in book 22 and his defeat of that compulsion in book 24. In this poem, we see Achilles as someone who has isolated himself from a supportive base of other human beings; who is enraged, murderously enraged by humiliation at the hands of his commanding officer; who is driven by the talionic impulse to exact vengeance indiscriminately from that officer and his army in its entirety; who is brought to the verge of suicide after suffering the death of his closest friend, who was serving as his surrogate in battle and who represented the one supportive human association he desperately needed; who is propelled to a berserk orgy of slaughter and the desecration of the corpse of his most hated enemy and the killer of his friend; and then who, in a radical reversal of the commitment to vengeance that has powered his actions for most of the *Iliad,* is relieved of his crushing burden of hatred by discovering the capacity within himself for redemptive compassion in his encounter with Priam in book 24.

In my view, the shield is Homer's commentary, subtle, indirect, and ironically incomprehensible to the one who will soon bear it in battle, on the relationship between the explosive, vindictive fury of Achilles's wrath and the healing virtue of his humane instincts which ultimately will triumph over it.

Taplin points out that this shield which is about to enter into bloody and gruesome battles of extreme intensity ought to, but does not, display the horrific emblems we find on other shields carried by warriors. He notes that the shield Agamemnon uses in fierce combat in book 11 has the face of the Gorgon on it as well as the figures of Fear and Terror. He cites the following scene inscribed on a hero's shield from the epic fragment, "The Shield of Heracles":

Leon Golden

> By them stood Darkness of Death, mournful and
> fearful, pale, shriveled, shrunk with hunger, swollen
> knees. Long nails tipped her hands, and she
> dribbled at the nose, and from her cheeks blood
> dripped down to the ground. She stood leering
> hideously, and much dust sodden with tears lay
> upon her shoulders.

The shield of Agamemnon and the shield of Heracles are
meant to strike terror in an enemy. The overwhelming majority of
scenes on the shield of Achilles have the opposite effect and we
must search for a persuasive explanation as to why a shield that
is destined to enter into furious combat should be embellished so
largely with peaceful rather than terrifying symbols. The following
remarks by Taplin contribute to the explanation for this situation:[25]

> The shield is a microcosm; but that does not mean
> it includes in miniature every single thing to be
> found in the world—that would be impossible, and
> is not in any case the way poetry and art work.
> They select and emphasize in order to impart
> meaning. The shield omits, for instance, poverty
> and misery; it omits trade and seafaring; it does
> not figure religion or cult, and it does not figure
> mythology or named heroes and places....the
> shield is a microcosm, not a utopia, and death
> and destruction are also there, though in inverse
> proportion to the rest of the Iliad. Rural life is
> invaded by the lions, and one of the two cities is
> surrounded by armies and carnage. I argued... that
> the city and its besiegers are meant to put us in
> mind of Troy and the Achaeans, in fact of the rest of
> the *Iliad*. What I now wish to suggest is that the city
> on the shield puts the *Iliad* itself into perspective;
> it puts war and prowess into perspective within
> the world as a whole. *On the shield the Iliad takes
> up, so to speak, one half of one of the five circles*
> (italics mine).

Understanding the Iliad

I think that Taplin is correct to read into the message of the five circles of the shield a commentary on the relationship between war and peace and about the potent but restricted role of war in the affairs of humanity, for the shield is, indeed, a microcosm of human existence; but the very special relationship which the shield has to Achilles should alert us to the fact that it there is a great probability that it carries a message encoded on it that applies directly to him. Because the scenes of peace on the shield significantly outweigh in number and emotional intensity the half-circle devoted to war, they lend weight to Owen's analysis, quoted by Taplin, that war "is only an incident in the busy world of human activities, that though Troy may fall and Achilles's life be wrecked, the world goes on as before."[26] We must focus sharply on the fact that this shield is not only the one "that Achilles will carry through the massacre of books 20 and 21 and which will avert Hector's last throw" (Taplin, p. 1), it is the device bearing affirmative messages of peaceful, joyous, and civilized life that, with the exception of one half of one of its five circles, contradicts the spirit of rage and revenge that governs the action of the poem from book 1 all the way to the desecration of the body of Hector in book 22. Let us see what the circles of the shield can communicate to us and to symbolize for Achilles.

The first circle on the shield, the innermost ring, devoted to the earth, the sky, the sea, the sun, the moon, and the constellations dwarf by their vastness of size and timelessness the human activities which take place in the circles which separate the cosmic bodies from the ocean in the outermost ring. War, hatred, vengeance, deaths in battle all take on a diminished presence in comparison to the depiction of cosmic bodies, so vast in size and longevity, that came into existence when the universe was born. Homer provides in the first and the final circles a sharp contrast between the vastness and permanence of nature and the limitations, variability, and transitoriness of the human condition. Taplin (p. 5) speaks of the astronomical bodies as the "cosmic constants and the markers of the passage of time reflected in Homer by recurrent formulae whatever the human vicissitudes they may accompany." The murderous, narcissistic rage of Achilles has caused tumultuous disasters for all who have come into contact with it, yet that rage and its disastrous consequences will shortly, in an instant, be dismissed by Achilles as a mistake

Leon Golden

that never should have happened. In book 19, Achilles says to Agamemnon:

> "Son of Atreus, was this better for both of us
> For you and me, when, grieved at heart, we raged
> In soul-devouring strife on account of a girl?
> I wish that Artemis had slain her with an arrow by
> the ships, on the day I captured her and destroyed
> Lyrnessus. Then not so many Achaians would
> have bitten the vast earth at the hands of their foes
> because of my great wrath. It was very profitable for
> Hector and the Trojans. But the Achaians I think will
> long remember our quarrel." (19.56-64)

Compared to the great and immutable forces of the cosmos obeying unbreakable laws of nature, human actions that have brought many to their knees and graves can in a moment be stripped of their original force and certainty, although pathetically not of their consequences, by the altered perspective on the part of those who have caused the disaster that it was all a mistake. Achilles and Agamemnon, in the aftermath of the death of a single soldier of special importance, can casually wave aside their enmity against each other which has consigned so many to death, to join forces in a campaign against an adversary who is now much more the object of their hatred than they had ever been to each other. Owen describes the situation well:[27]

> In the case of Achilles, one feels by the careless
> indifference with which he dismisses the subject
> how utterly insignificant the whole business of
> Briseis and his quarrel has become. Because of this
> "girl," of whom he speaks so contemptuously now,
> he has almost brought the whole Achaean cause to
> irreparable disaster. Hundreds of good men have
> perished who might be alive now, as he himself
> notes....The sublime arrogance of his attitude is
> brilliantly thrown into relief by the preceding picture
> of the wounded chieftains painfully limping into the
> assembly...It is to such men, Homer thus makes us
> realize, that these words are addressed—to men
> who in the peril caused by his action have valiantly

Understanding the Iliad

been facing death, and bear on their bodies the marks of that desperate struggle. There is not a trace of shame or apology in his words....he has no sense of guilt...

From the first circle of the shield, a lesson in humility can emerge as we focus on human fallibility within the context of the vastness of nature's universe. It is a lesson that Achilles will not learn until books 23 and 24.

The second circle represents two cities, one at peace and one at war. In the city at peace, we find a marriage celebration and the arbitration of a legal case. For Taplin (pp. 5-6) the wedding celebration is occasion for the enjoyment of the "good life" accompanied by joyful "singing and dancing which...epitomize the pleasures of peace." The arbitration scene for Taplin depicts "the stable justice of a civilized city." In the city at war, we have two armies engaged in pressing and defending against a siege. I believe that we can see in the contrasting mood of the two cities a reflection and a foreshadowing of different dimensions of Achilles's evolved and evolving character. In the city at peace, we observe weddings and festivals in which:

They were leading brides from their rooms with gleaming Torches through the city, and the bridal song, loud and strong, Rose up. And young men, whirled in a dance, and among them flutes and lyres sounded forth. And the women, each one, Stood at their doorway and admired them. (18.492-96)

In the city at war we see soldiers

Striking each other with bronze-tipped spears. Among them joining in war were Strife and Battle Tumult and Death the Destroyer, holding one man alive, newly wounded, And another unwounded, and another, dead, she dragged through the battle by his feet. And the cloak she had about her shoulders was red with the blood of men. (18.534-38)

Leon Golden

In the city at peace, we find two men engaged in a quarrel about blood money for a murder and seeking an arbitrator to resolve their dispute:

> And the people were applauding, encouraging both
> sides, But heralds held them back. And the elders
> sat On polished stones in the sacred circle, holding
> in Their hands the scepters of loud-voiced heralds.
> Then they darted up in their midst and gave
> judgments alternately And there lay in the middle
> two talents of gold to give to the one Who spoke
> among them the straightest judgment. (18.502-08)

Through book 22, we can identify Achilles with the city at war as he rages against Agamemnon and Hector with "Hate, Din, and the Angel of Death" at his side and like the Angel of Death his clothes will run red with human blood when he returns to war in book 20. After book 22, we can identify Achilles with the city at peace as he acts as an arbitrator and pacifier during the minor disputes, displays of temper, and conflicts among contestants which erupt during the funeral games for Patroclus in book 23 and so assumes a function not unlike the elders on the shield who hold the staves of heralds and will be rewarded with gold for giving the straightest judgment. Although Achilles never achieves the state of joyfulness represented in the wedding scene on the second circle, the tenderness with which he treats Hector's body as he returns it to his father, and the compassion and affection with which he embraces Priam in their shared intensity of grief and admiration for each other in book 24, establishes an affirmative emotional analog to the mood of the city of peace. After the orgy of slaughter in books 20-22, a most fierce enactment of the *lex talionis,* a law, psychiatrists tell us, that is subversive to civilized life, the humane interaction in book 24 of Achilles with Priam and the honor Achilles shows Hector through his respectful arrangements for his funeral harmonize well with the human condition in its most enlightened state, which is a function of the city of peace, not the city of war.

Taplin analyzes the third circle as one devoted to rural life and divided into the four seasons of the year. The scene in spring is one of plowmen "driving their teams up and down rows" and when they come to the end of the field, "a man would run up and hand them a cup of sweet wine" (18.585-87). It is a scene filled with the

Understanding the Iliad

pleasure of the rewarding labor of working rich land, and the joy felt in the activity is symbolized by the description of the field which "was black behind them, just as if plowed, and yet it was gold, all gold, forged to a wonder" (18.589-91).

The joyous life of peace continues to unfold through vistas of activities taking place in summer. We have here a scene involving the reaping, collecting, and binding of the crop. The scene is enriched with details that add delight to the work taking place in the field. When the reapers cut the grain, handfuls fall to the ground, while the binders tie the rest into sheaves. Young children stand by and make a game of gathering up the grain that has fallen and eagerly giving it to the binders. Among all this activity, the king stands by rejoicing in his heart at all of this happy and profitable activity. We then see heralds and women preparing a feast for both the king and the workers. This summer scene contains more pleasurable details than the one that preceded it in the springtime. The rhythmic activity of reapers and binders, the cheerful children offering assistance, the happy king surveying his domain, and the preparation of an abundant meal to satisfy the needs of those who have worked so hard during the day all combine to create a scene suffused with the gentle joy of productive, happy labor as part of daily life.

The events of autumn follow, and we are given a happy picture of the gathering of the grapes presented within the magnificent workmanship of the shield. Young girls and boys in joyous spirits carry the honey-sweet fruit in wicker baskets, while among them, a boy sings beautifully, in a delicate voice, the Linos song of lament. The others dancing in unison with singing and shouts of joy follow along skipping through the vineyard.

The passage which follows, Taplin suggests, should represent winter since the others are clearly identifiable as spring, summer, and autumn. It describes herdsmen and their dogs trying to protect their flocks from attack by marauding lions, and it indicates the discipline and courage needed to preserve the peacetime farm from the ravages of wild animals. It is important to note that the efforts of the herdsman are productive, not destructive, as in war as they seek to defend what hard work has earned for them. The scene adds a realistic note that provides some balance to the joyful celebrations of agricultural life we have seen up to now.

The fourth circle of the shield celebrates the ecstatic happiness of youth through the grand spectacle of a joyful dance.

Leon Golden

On a magnificent dance floor, radiant young men and beautiful young women buoyantly express their life-affirming spirit in the intricate and elegant dance movements they execute. Their exquisite, graceful animation and their splendid clothing and adornments delight the audience, which surrounds them as two acrobats leaping among them enhance this dazzling ritual of youthful hopefulness and exuberance. We should not ignore any detail of Homer's description.

> On it the famed lame god skillfully wrought an
> arena For dancing such as the one once in wide
> Cnosus Daedalus fashioned for fair-haired Ariadne.
> Young men and girls worth many oxen Were
> dancing there, holding hands at each other's wrists.
> Of these the girls wore fine linen, and the men well-
> woven tunics softly shining with oil. And the girls
> had beautiful floral crowns and the men Had golden
> knives hanging from silver belts. They were running
> with knowing feet, very lightly, As when some potter
> sitting at the wheel that is fitted To his hands tests
> it to see if it will spin. And at times They ran in rows
> with each other. And a great Crowd stood around
> the lovely dance Rejoicing; and two acrobats were
> whirling In the midst of them leading the festivities.
> (18.590-606)

This is the last ring of the shield that depicts aspects of mortal existence and brings into sharp focus the shield's affirmative vision of human life. Taplin is surely right (p. 9) that "the length and unity of this scene make it appear the climax of the whole shield." This climax contains within it a pointed irony, for the shield's festive dance of life will yield shortly to a morbid ballet of death on the Trojan battlefield.

At a moment, then, of great prominence in the poem, Homer has inserted an elaborate description of Achilles's shield that stands in contradiction to the mood and tone of the events that take place through book 22. The *Iliad,* however, does not reach its completion in books 20-22. At a critical phase in the poem, as Achilles is about to rejoin the Achaian army and embark on a pursuit of vengeance most fierce, the shield captures our attention with its eloquent foreshadowing of the real climax of the *Iliad.* It

Understanding the Iliad

guides us beyond the massacre of Hector to the final twenty-three days of the poem during which books 23 and 24 unfold, where the civilized and ennobling virtues of cities at peace soar into ascendancy over vengeance taken in narcissistic wrath through the furious slaughter meted out in war.

Book 19 is a venue in which we see the anger of Achilles rekindled and mounting to a new intensity. When Thetis delivers the magnificent armor forged by Hephaestus:

> Trembling then took hold of all the Myrmidons nor
> could anyone bear to look Straight at the armor but
> they dreaded it. However, When Achilles saw it,
> wrath overcame him Even more and beneath their
> lids his Two eyes flashed terribly as if flaming fire.
> (19.14-17)

In a speech of reconciliation, Agamemnon announces that he will bestow on Achilles all of the prizes his envoys had promised to him earlier. To Achilles, the gifts which he feels he deserves have now become a trivial matter. They are, he says, Agamemnon's concern; war is what is on his mind, and so great is his rage, so great his appetite for vengeance that he wishes to rush immediately into battle. Both Odysseus and Agamemnon interfere at this point and argue that it is impossible to send the army into combat without adequate food and rest. To this cautionary advice about the preparation of an army for war that is based on the realistic considerations of military commanders, Achilles replies:

> "Most glorious son of Atreus, king of men,
> Agamemnon, You ought rather at some other time
> to concern yourself with these matters, when there
> is a pause in the war—And the rage in my breast
> is not so great. But now they lie savaged whom
> Hector, the son of Priam, Struck dead when Zeus
> granted him glory. And you urge us to eat? Truly
> now I would bid the sons of The Achaians to go to
> war fasting and without food And at the setting of
> the sun make a great feast when we have atoned
> for our disgrace." (19.199-208)

Leon Golden

Odysseus's and Agamemnon's realistic vision of what is required for the army to fight prevails here against the immense fury of Achilles, which is sufficient in itself to energize him for the slaughter that is to take place. Achilles resists all efforts to mollify his grief and rage and Homer tells us that "no pleasure was in his heart until he plunged into the bloody mouth of war (19.312-13). At this point, there is only one therapy Achilles can envision for himself, and that is punitive vengeance inflicted on the battlefield. We see the intensity of his appetite for retribution in Homer's description of Achilles arming himself with the weapons newly fashioned by Hephaestus:

> There was a gnashing of his teeth
> And his two eyes flashed like blazing fire,
> And unbearable grief entered his
> Heart; then with rage against the Trojans
> He put on the gifts of the god that Hephaestus
> Had toiled to make for him. (19.365-68)

At the end of book 19, furious desire for revenge still dominates Achilles's actions; only now, with Hector as its object instead of Agamemnon, it has been elevated to a much higher level of ferocity. Even the eerie warning his horse, Xanthus, gives him that his death is not far off does not alter his mood or resolve. We have seen how callously he consigned his own allies to death in the shadow of his quarrel with Agamemnon, and how lightly this rested on his conscience when he returned to the Achaian fold to exact revenge from Hector. Now Achilles is about to descend into the abyss of human degradation on the killing fields of Troy where, without compassion, without humanity, he will pollute the landscape with rivers of blood. Schein makes the important observation:[28]

> From 20.378 to the death of Hector in Book 22, no other mortal on either side kills an enemy. In Book 20 Achilles kills fifteen Trojans in succession, six with blows to the head or neck—a much higher proportion of such wounds than usual. He is utterly ruthless, with neither patience for supplicants nor inclination to spare life. He has virtually ceased to be human both physically and ethically; he

Understanding the Iliad

has become a force of sheer destructive energy, annihilating whatever gets in his way.

Iphition, the son of Otrynteus, is the first recipient of this savagery. We are told that Achilles split his head in two as Iphition charged him and then drove his spear through the helmet and temple of Demoleon, crushing the brain within the skull. Achilles then kills Hippodamas with a spear thrust to his back that sent him bellowing like a bull to his death. After that, he goes after Priam's youngest son, Polydorus, hitting him in the back as he raced by and opening a wound in his stomach from which the internal organs spurt. Afterwards, Achilles kills four Trojans in succession with his spear and sword: Dryups, Demuchus, Lagonus, and Dardanus. Next it is Tros's turn to die who foolishly supposes that he might convince Achilles to spare his life:

> ...He was attempting to touch his knees with his hands Desiring to entreat him, but Achilles thrust his sword Into his liver; the liver slipped out And black blood filled his bosom as darkness covered His eyes and his breathing stopped. (20.468-72)

There is no stopping point in the escalating ferocity of Achilles's hunger for vengeance as one Trojan after another dies brutally:

> ...And standing close he wounded Mulius striking his ear with his spear; and the bronze spear-point went straight through the other ear. And he struck Echechlus, son of Agenor, in the middle of his head with his hilted sword, and the whole sword grew warm with blood, and dark death and Mighty fate clouded over his eyes. Then Deucalion, where the tendons of the elbow come together, him he pierced through the arm with his bronze spear-point, and Deucalion waited Looking at death before him with his arm hanging heavy. And Achilles struck his neck with his sword and drove Far off his head and helmet together. And the Marrow spurted up from his spine and he lay stretched out on the ground. (20.472-83)

Leon Golden

Homer's suggestive symbol of Achilles's fury at this time is of unnatural fire raging through deep glens of a parched mountain as the deep forest burns and the wind, driving the flame in wild confusion, whirls it in every direction as the black earth is awash with human blood (20.490-94). Achilles continues his massacre of Trojans in book 21 as Homer tells us:

> ...When his hands grew tired of slaughter He
> selected twelve youths alive from the river As
> retribution for the slaying of Patroclus, son of
> Menoetius. These he led forth dazed as fawns, and
> he bound their Hands behind them with the finely
> cut leather belts Which they wore around their pliant
> tunics. These he gave to his comrades to lead back
> to the hollow ships. And then rushed back again
> eager to kill. (21.26-33)

His next encounter is with a son of Priam, Lycaon, who once before had been captured by Achilles and was sold, at that time, for a high price. Now he becomes a suppliant to Achilles and pleads for mercy and the chance to be ransomed once again. Achilles's mood has turned completely hard and brutal after Patroclus's death, and Lycaon heard a cruel voice telling him not to speak of ransom or plead (21.99-100). After telling Lycaon that Patroclus—a better man than he—has died, and that Achilles himself is also destined to die, Lycaon realizes that his fate is sealed and confronts a death that comes by means of a savage stroke of Achilles's sword to the trunk of his body. Then:

> Achilles took hold of him by his foot and sent him
> Flying into the river. With a curse he spoke winged
> words: "Lie there with the fish who will lick the blood
> From your wounds, and care nothing for you. Your
> mother Will not lay you on a bier and lament, but
> eddying Scamander will carry you into the broad
> bosom of the sea, And a fish leaping over a wave
> will dart up on the black Rippling water and eat
> Lycaon's shining fat. So do you perish until we
> come to the city Of holy Ilios, you fleeing and I
> slaughtering you From behind. (21.120-29)

Understanding the Iliad

After the death of Lycaon, Achilles goes on an orgy of devastation that chokes the waters of the river. The slaughter is so vast that Homer cannot describe it in human terms but has recourse to symbolism from the world of nature to characterize Achilles's unbridled fury. He gives the River Scamander a human presence who rebels against the murderous onslaught of Achilles that is stifling and polluting his waters with a demand that the bloody holocaust cease. When the pleas of Scamander are to no avail, the river attacks Achilles with its swirling waters and seeks to drown him as he flees in terror of this supernatural assault. As his courage begins to fail him and he envisions a useless, unheroic death by drowning, Poseidon and Athena come to his aid and summon Hephaestus to pit all the force of voracious fire against the deadly, churning waters of the river. What follows then is a colossal struggle between water and fire until the strength of the river fails and Scamander asks Hera to impose a truce that permits Achilles to continue his slaughter of Trojans. With his fury unabated, Achilles then causes the Trojans to stampede into the safety of their city. The clashing forces of water and fire, the violence of nature in its untrammeled fury, is the mechanism that Homer chooses, the only one sufficient, for evoking for us the inhuman, murderous rage of Achilles.

The climax of all of this furious pursuit of vengeance comes, of course, in book 22 with the killing of Hector and the mutilation of his corpse. In his dying moments, after being slain by Achilles, Hector seeks to arrange a civilized outcome that would permit his burial with honor:

> "I beg you by your life and knees And by your parents, do not allow the dogs to Devour me by the ships of the Achaians. But do You accept gold and bronze in abundance, gifts My father and royal mother will give you, And send my body back home in order that the Trojans And their wives may honor my death with fire. (22.338-43)

Achilles's answer to this plea is:

> "Don't beseech me, dog, by my knees and parents. I wish that my wrath and fury would let me Carve up

Leon Golden

> your flesh and eat it raw because of the things you
> have done; there is no one Who might ward off the
> dogs from your head, Not even if they bring here
> ten or twenty times the ransom And weigh them out
> and promise even more, Not even if Priam, son of
> Dardanus, should bid to ransom You for your weight
> in gold, not then will your royal mother Who bore
> you place you on a bier and lament you But dogs
> and birds will totally devour you." (22.345-54)

And then there is a concluding act of brutal degradation that Achilles's rage drives him to commit against Hector in fulfillment of the talionic impulse that was provoked into action by the quarrel with Agamemnon in book 1 and energized into raw fury by the death of Patroclus in book 16:

> He spoke and devised unseemly treatment for
> God-like Hector. He bore through the tendons of
> both feet
> From behind from heel to ankle and fastened them
> with ox-hide
> Straps and tied them to his chariot, and allowed
> Hector's head to
> Drag behind. And having mounted his chariot
> And having lifted the glorious armor onto it
> He whipped his horses on and not unwillingly did
> the pair fly.
> And a cloud of dust arose from the body as it was
> dragged
> And about him his dark hair trailed and his head lay
> completely
> Covered by dust, the head that once was so
> handsome;
> But now Zeus gave him over to his foes to be
> abused
> In his native land. (22.395-04)

The war that Achilles has waged in books 20-22 has been much more a personal vendetta than a manifestation of courage in the heroic code mode. The many deaths he inflicts in rapid and continuous succession constitute a berserk killing spree dedicated

Understanding the Iliad

to his own individual quest for a vengeance that will assuage his emotional pain. The horrific treatment of the corpse of Hector is almost the last act of extreme degradation on Achilles's part—one more is yet to come—but it shows Achilles in his darkest hour before the process of redemption sets in. Owen describes the condition of Achilles at this point well:[29]

> In the words that pass between Achilles and the dying Hector nothing can be clearer than the poet's intention. There is not a trace here of anything noble in Achilles....This is sheer unrelieved revenge without a spark of any other feeling to lighten it. All other feelings seem dead....Bk XXII shows us the wrath of Achilles at its blackest....For the heart of the Iliad is the tragedy of Achilles. So he gives us without flinching and without qualification the full horror of hatred working in a soul capable of the extremes of passion.

Critics of the *Iliad* have come a long way in their assessment of the poem from Monro's judgment concerning books 23 and 24 that:[30]

> 1. Neither of the books in question can be said to be necessary to the poetical completeness of the Iliad. The events of the twenty-second book bring the story to a conclusion, which—to a modern reader at least—leaves nothing to be desired. The anger of Achilles is appeased, his vengeance is satisfied, the danger to the Greeks has passed away. Hence, as Mr. Grote argued, "the death of Hector satisfies the exigencies of a coherent scheme, and we are not entitled to extend the oldest poem beyond the limit which necessity prescribes."
> 2. The two books do not stand well together. They seem to represent two different ways of bringing the poem to an end....While there might have been room (artistically speaking) for one last book— either the Funeral Games or the Ransoming of Hector—there is not room for both.

Leon Golden

Monro's and Grote's *Iliad* is purely and simply an adventure story filled with the physical violence of war and vengeance that achieves its dramatic and thrilling completion with the brutal desecration of the corpse of Hector. This is a view that is in direct opposition to the interpretation I have been presenting that the *Iliad* is a *Bildungsroman*, which, although taking place in the context of war and combat is, in reality, a drama of inner turmoil, struggle, and psychological and emotional evolution. Achilles's most important victory is not won by massacres on the plains of Troy but by his triumph over himself, over the controlling force of narcissistic rage and over his bondage to the *lex talionis*. From this point of view, books 23 and 24 are absolutely essential to the meaning and purpose of the *Iliad*.

Owen and Schein both recognize a different Achilles emerging in book 23. Owen notes specific acts of tact and affection on Achilles's part which he correctly states are there "to make the transition from the Achilles of Book XXII to the Achilles of Book XXIV."[31] Schein writes:[32]

> In the funeral games he holds in honor of Patroklos, Achilles' mood seems to change to a controlled, detached sociability. After spending so much of the previous twenty-two books in hatred and conflict, he does not compete himself but gracefully and peacefully resolves disputes between Ajax son of Oileus and Idomeneus and between Antilochos and Menelaos, as well as the wrestling match between Telamonian Ajax and Odysseus. Himself deprived of a prize and honor early in the poem, he now awards extra prizes and honor to Nestor and Eumelos, and a first prize to Agamemnon, in a courtly and considerate fashion, so as to avoid disappointment or difficulty. Homer here modulates, as it were, between the inconsolable, hateful Achilles of Books 18-23 and the humane Achilles of the scene with Priam.

It is Schein's view also, however, at the conclusion of his discussion of books 23 and 24 that[33]

Understanding the Iliad

...Achilles is not changed into a new and different character, either because of some inward, spiritual growth or on account of his reintegration into the human community. Rather, he is reestablished as his distinctive self—as the hero with capacities for both *philotês* [love] and *mênis* [wrath] he was at the beginning of Book 1. The sympathy he shows Priam is the same sympathy that led him to summon the assembly at 1.54 in an attempt to find an end to the plague.

Earlier in his study, however, Schein wrote:[34]

But the character of Achilles is not constant. In order to understand his role in the *Iliad*, it is necessary to go through the poem from beginning to end, noting both the stages of Achilles' responses to the situations he finds himself in and the poet's sequence of causes and effects that forms the setting for Achilles' attempt to explain himself. *The poem presents an evolving Achilles* [italics mine] out of whose initial resentment and later vacillation develops his unique absoluteness.

With the assistance of psychoanalytical insight, and the close reading of the text I have pursued, I think that it should not be difficult to demonstrate that Achilles is not seriously conflicted with wrath *and* love from books 1-22 but that narcissistic injury arising from his humiliation by Agamemnon and the rage resulting from it *alone* directs his actions until the death of Patroclus; thereafter we observe, as a direct consequence of the loss of the one person who, after his alienation from the Achaian army, prevents his total isolation from the human community, an uncontrolled intensification of his wrath and lust for vengeance that leads to the brutal slaughter of Trojans at the Scamander River and the inhumane mutilation of the body of Hector. Achilles's enormous revenge does not, however, quell his psychic pain and it is *only* in books 23 and 24 that he seeks relief and redemption by replacing the impotent force of rage with the healing power of compassion. Thus I believe that Schein's original recognition of an *evolving Achilles* represents the correct interpretation of the hero's role in

Leon Golden

the *Iliad* and I would like to follow his suggestion and review the critical events of the poem that bear on the question of Achilles's emotional state, his alleged manifestations of love, and his very real demonstrations of hate, up to the end of book 22.

It has been suggested that Achilles calls an assembly to find the cause of the plague that is afflicting the army because of his love for his fellow soldiers. It is certainly possible that their suffering affects him although *all* that he actually says, *all* that Homer attributes to him in the poem's text is:

> "Son of Atreus, now I think that we will return home,
> Wandering back, if indeed we should escape
> death, if war and pestilence together will defeat the
> Achaians." (1.59-61)

It is true that in the lines just preceding this passage, we are told that Hera suggested the idea of an assembly to Achilles because "she cared for the Greeks and it pained her/to see them dying." There is no doubt about the goddess's concern for the dying Greeks, for she makes that point explicitly, but Achilles does not repeat her words, and all we can surmise from Achilles's actual statement is a concern that the expedition will have to be scrapped because of the continuing casualties the army is incurring. At the end of this passage, at the conclusion of the quarrel with Agamemnon, no one surely could find love as a factor in his attitude the army. He looks forward to Agamemnon's remorse over his actions toward him after he abandons the army and the war and "many fall dead at the hands of man-slaying Hector" (1.2421-43). Achilles may have been opposed to sacrificing Achaian soldiers to the plague, but he is all too willing to sacrifice them to his rage against Agamemnon and that certainly does not equate with the emotion of love. It has been suggested that Achilles expresses love in his relationship with his mother, Thetis. Yet in his conversation with Thetis in book 1, lines 364-412, it is she who expresses compassion for him; he is exclusively concerned with the insult he has received and his desire for revenge. He asks Thetis to become the agent of that revenge by negotiating with Zeus, who is indebted to her, and tells her to remind him of his obligation and

Understanding the Iliad

"To see if he may be willing to help the Trojans And to hem the Achaians in around their sterns. And the sea, while they are being slain, So that all may profit from their king and the son of Atreus, wide-Ruling Agamemnon, may recognize his madness Because he did not honor the best of all the Fighting Achaeans." (1.408-12)

It is Achilles's intention to take revenge on Agamemnon by killing off soldiers in his army. This is hardly a manifestation of love for his Achaian allies. In book 9, Achilles greets an embassy from Agamemnon as those dearest to him, but he denies their pleas that he come to their aid before they are destroyed by Hector. He announces first that he is going home the next day and will leave them to their dire fate and later he says no, he will stay but not lift a finger to help them until Hector has slashed a murderous path through all the ships and camp, killing the Achaians on his way up to where the Myrmidons are stationed. Then, after many have died, he will finally enter the war and protect his own forces. His repeated willingness to see many Achaians perish as punishment for Agamemnon can hardly be described as love for the army. It has been argued that Achilles shows love for Phoenix. In book 9, however, when Phoenix, his foster father, pleads with Achilles to accept the gifts from Agamemnon and return to the war, Achilles tells him to stop pleading on behalf of Agamemnon but to hate him since he hates him and he will not allow Phoenix friendship with both of them. I do not detect any nuance of love in this command to Phoenix to abandon his own feelings of patriotism and sense or what is right and wrong and slavishly obey Achilles's priorities. At the end of book 9, when the embassy brings its gloomy news back to Agamemnon and the Achaian camp, Diomedes does not remind the army of a once-compassionate Achilles with whom they might still negotiate. Instead he says it was a mistake to plead with him and send gifts because Achilles's arrogance was sufficient without the incentive of Agamemnon's rewards.

In book 11, Achilles is a spectator rejoicing to see the casualties taken by the Achaian army, and remarks to Patroclus "Now I think the Achaians will be standing about my knees, begging me" (11.609-10). It is clear that Achilles feels no sympathy for the suffering Achaians, but rather, takes pleasure in the casualties they incur, for that contributes to his purpose

Leon Golden

of punishing and humiliating Agamemnon. There is no evidence here for Achilles's love of the army. In book 16, Achilles grants Patroclus's request that he be permitted to wear Achilles's armor and enter the war in order to drive back the dominating Trojans. He is concerned that Patroclus survive the battle, and advises him to rout the Trojans but not to risk his life by attempting to capture the city of Troy. Surely, there is concern for Patroclus here, but there is just as much, or even more, concern for his own opportunity for glory. He warns Patroclus to return from combat after driving the Trojans away from the Achaian ships and not seek the larger prize of Troy, itself, because any success he has against the Trojans will diminish his own honor. Then he utters the harsh prayer we have discussed earlier and which very much bears repeating now:

> "I pray to Father Zeus and Athena and Apollo
> That not one of the Trojans might escape death,
> As many as they are, nor any of the Argives,
> But that the two of us would survive
> In order that we alone, might tear down Troy's
> Sacred battlements." (16.97-100)

This prayer is certainly not consistent with the love of one's comrades, but it is all too consistent with the narcissistic temperament that privileges grandiosity and insensitivity to the feelings of others. Finally, in book 19, we have the reconciliation between Achilles and Agamemnon. Achilles, as we have mentioned previously, says that their quarrel over a girl was meaningless and he now wishes she had died before he took her captive, for:

> "Then not so many Achaians would have bitten the
> vast earth at the hands of their foes because of my
> great wrath. It was very profitable for Hector and the
> Trojans. But the Achaians I think will long remember
> our quarrel." (19.61-64)

Thus does Achilles dismiss a dispute that brought devastation to the Achaian army and, as Owen has pointed out, "hundreds of good men have perished who might be alive now, as he himself notes," but there is not a word of apology, admission of guilt, or expression of pity for the comrades who have been the victims of

Understanding the Iliad

his rage, a rage that is now dismissed as irrelevant. The absence of these signs of sorrow and responsibility clearly tells us that up to this point, Achilles has never felt an emotion kindred to love for the Achaian army. He has exclusively pursued his own interest and his own interest has been vengeance, pure and simple, for the implementation of which he has been willing to victimize all who could serve his vindictive agenda including the entire Achaian army. We see the focus on his own self-interest further in book 19 when, as noted previously, he expresses his desire to lead the army into the field against Hector immediately, without food, without rest. Odysseus and Agamemnon prevent this from happening, but we see again that his concern is not with the well-being of the army, but with the satisfaction of his insatiable appetite for revenge.

It is my view that a new and radically changed Achilles does emerge by the end of book 24 and that the process of transition from Achilles, furiously in pursuit of vengeance, to Achilles, emancipated from the corrosive addiction to the talionic impulse, begins in book 23. Why and how this transition takes place and becomes the essential theme of the *Iliad* is the triumph of the genius and art of Homer.

There are three focal points for the action of book 23: (1) the appearance of Patroclus in a dream to Achilles; (2) the burial rites for Patroclus; and (3) and the funeral games for Patroclus. The acceptance of the finality of the death of Patroclus is the first step that Achilles must take in coming to closure with grief for his friend whose existence provided the only access to the human community he needed to survive and thrive. We recall Alexander Lowen's description of the narcissist as someone who even if he or she "doesn't acquire a flock of followers...must have at least one devotee, whether a lover or prostitute. In other words [they] must have someone who needs them. They cannot be alone. And the relationship must be one in which they have control." Achilles has been protected, temporarily, from the dismal reality that he is now alone because the rage which overmastered him when Hector slew Patroclus was translated into a vast storm of destructive energy that occupied every aspect of his being as he massacred Trojans on the battlefield and subjected Hector's corpse to horrific desecration. At the conclusion of the dream in which he sees a vision of Patroclus:

Leon Golden

> ...He reached out with his hands But did not grasp him. The spirit, like smoke, departed Beneath the earth, with a shrill cry. (23.99-101)

Achilles now recognizes that the physical existence of Patroclus is, once and for all, over. There remains then the task of funeral rites for him, to which Achilles now turns his attention. These rites, as might be expected, are elaborate. They culminate with the sacrifice of animals and men:

> He set down two-handled amphoras of honey and oil Leaning them against the bier and, groaning loudly, he rapidly Hurled four horses with high, arching necks onto the pyre. Nine dogs of the prince fed at his table and of these He cut the throats of two and thrust them on the pyre, And also twelve noble sons of the great-hearted Trojans, Killing them with bronze and planning cruel deeds. (23.170-76)

The slaughter of the twelve Trojan warriors, on which Richardson aptly comments that "clearly attention is being drawn to the exceptional savagery of this action,"[35] is the next to the last time that Achilles physically inflicts such brutality in the poem, although his wrath is still so great that he announces his intention to the spirit of Patroclus to feed Hector's body not to the fire that ennobles heroes, but to the dogs for his ultimate disgrace.

After the Achaians prepare for the burial of Patroclus in accordance with Achilles's instructions, they start to leave the site, but Achilles

> Held the army back and made them sit in a wide assembly and he brought forth prizes from his ships, Cauldrons and tripods and horses and mules, and powerful Oxen, and fair-girdled women, and grey iron. (23.258-61)

These are the prizes for the funeral games which Achilles will now sponsor and which complete the action of book 23. Some critics have felt that the transition from the burial of Patroclus to the funeral games is strangely brief but with the help of Lowen's

Understanding the Iliad

comments, I think we have a realistic and persuasive explanation for Achilles's immediate commencement of these games. In discussing the psychological profile of narcissism, Lowen has called attention to characteristics such as rage, insensitivity to the feelings of others, and grandiosity—all characteristics we have observed in Achilles. Achilles's blind rage that drives his lust for vengeance is obvious as the factor dictating the action of the first twenty-two books of the poem; his insensitivity to the feelings of others is especially clear in book 9, where he ignores the earnest pleas for help of those he loves best in the Achaian army, and in books 20-22 where, with brutality and often sarcasm, he wreaks vengeance, even inflicting mutilation on his enemies; and his grandiosity is especially visible in the certainty he expresses to Patroclus that the Achaians must now cower before him because of the casualties they have sustained and his prayer to the most potent of deities that both Achaians and Trojans disappear from the face of the earth, in order to satisfy his impulse for revenge.

We recall that Lowen has told us that it is a characteristic of narcissistic individuals that, while they do not need the support of a mass of followers, they must have at least one person who needs them—"they cannot be alone." With the death of Patroclus, Achilles has lost his supportive human contact but, by implementing the strategy of the funeral games, he immediately discovers a means for reestablishing with the Achaian army a relationship that was undermined because of his total insensitivity to the feelings and needs of his allies. Achilles resumes a role among his Achaian comrades not only because he must have human contact, important as that is, but also because with the death of Patroclus, Achilles experiences, for the first time in the poem, a choking sense of total helplessness in the face of unrecoverable loss. Rage, vengeance, insensitivity to the feelings of others, and the grandiose image of himself as capable of enforcing his intentions in any and all circumstances empowered him in the past to meet any impediment to his will with arrogant confidence. He could threaten Agamemnon with possible death, he could condemn the Achaian army to immense suffering and losses to satisfy his vengeance, he could sling the slaughtered Lycaon into the Scamander for the fish to devour, he could inhumanely brutalize the corpse of Hector. He faced the world, since he needed no human friendship or support other than that of Patroclus, without the troubling emotions of sadness and fear,

Leon Golden

that is, he faced the world shielded by an image of invulnerability. Lowen has some penetrating comments on those who manifest this condition:[36]

> In the preceding chapter we saw that narcissism develops from the denial of feeling. Although the denial of feeling affects all feeling, two emotions in particular are subject to severe inhibition—sadness and fear. They are singled out because their expression makes the person feel vulnerable. To express sadness leads to an awareness of loss and evokes longing. To long for someone or to need someone leaves the person open to possible rejection and humiliation. Not wanting or not feeling desire is a defense against possible hurt. The denial of fear has a similar objective. If one doesn't feel afraid, one doesn't feel vulnerable; presumably, one can't be hurt. The denial of sadness and fear enables the person to project an image of independence, courage, and strength. This image hides the person's vulnerability from him-or herself and from others. The image, however, is only a façade and therefore impotent.

While Achilles has not and will not feel fear, he has experienced and will continue to experience until the end of the poem, sadness and longing and, therefore, will come to know increasingly in books 23 and 24 that he has not escaped the shared mortal vulnerability to the pathos of human existence. It will be deeply ingrained in him that, in Lowen's words quoted earlier, "there are many instances in which we are not the masters of our fate—yet our helplessness in these areas is tolerable because all human beings are in the same boat. And we need each other to counter the darkness, to keep out the cold, to provide meaning to existence." Achilles's interaction with the Achaian warriors who are contestants in the games is his initial opportunity to draw strength from the common human limitations and vulnerability they all share and to which he mistakenly felt immune until the death of Patroclus.

The first contest is a chariot race, during the course of which a trivial dispute that threatens to turn violent arises between

Understanding the Iliad

Idomeneus and Ajax, son of Oïleus, over who is leading in the race. Before the heated words of the two warriors lead to serious physical injury, Achilles intervenes:

> "No longer respond to each other with harsh words,
> Ajax and Idomeneus, it is not fitting for you to do
> so. You would be Indignant with another, whoever
> might do such things. But do you Sit down in our
> assembly and keep watching the horses. Soon
> they Themselves in their eager haste for victory will
> come before you And then each of you will know
> which horse is first and which Second." (23.492-98)

Achilles, with the experience of the terrible consequences of his own quarrel with Agamemnon behind him, now gives the kind of advice to disputants that he was unable to take himself from Nestor in book 1. He appears before us, like the arbitrators in the city of peace on his shield, acting to mediate a dispute rather than inflame it. First prize goes to Diomedes, who wins the race, and next in order come Antilochus, Menelaus, Meriones, and last of all Eumelos, "a pitiful figure," as Richardson says, "dragging his chariot behind him, driving his horses in front, and he evokes Akhilleus' pity."[37] It is at 23.534 in the Greek text that Homer explicitly says that Achilles "pitied" Eumelus when he saw the sorry state he was in, and to alleviate his embarrassment, he offers to give him second prize although he most certainly has not earned it. Achilles did not express pity for the soldiers dying of the plague in book 1 (although Hera did); he did not feel pity for the fate that he threatened to impose on the Greeks he loved best in book 9. He did not pity the victims of his savage vengeance in books 20-22 or the mutilated corpse of Hector, and he did not feel pity—just the opposite—for the twelve young Trojan soldiers whom he slew and hurled upon the funeral pyre of Patroclus just before the funeral games began. I do not recall that previous to this time the word "pity" was ever applied to an emotion experienced by Achilles, or that up to now, pity was ever unambiguously expressed by him as demonstrated by a specific reference in the text except, by implication, in his cautionary advice to Patroclus not to risk death when routing the Trojans.

Antilochus, who actually came in second in the race, objects to losing his rightful prize just because Achilles pities Eumelus,

Leon Golden

and again the explicit Greek word for "pity" is used by Antilochus here. If Eumelus is dear to Achilles's heart, then Antilochus says he should produce a new prize for him from the large stone of valuable items in his hut and not strip another warrior of something he deserves. The reader is struck by a rough parallelism between Antilochus's situation here and Achilles's circumstances in book 1. Achilles suggests subjecting Antilochus to the same unfair treatment that he suffered at the hands of Agamemnon—the unjustifiable loss of a prize he had earned. We do not know if that parallel was on Achilles's mind or not but we do know that Achilles "smiled" (23.555) because he liked Antilochus and accedes to his request.

Again, I cannot think of another, previous instance in the poem when Achilles was transported to such an amicable and tranquil mood that anyone was the happy recipient of his "smile"; not Agamemnon in books 1, 9, and 23; not Thetis in book 1 (before whom he sorrowfully weeps); not the supplicant embassy from Agamemnon in book 9 whose pleas he rejects out of hand; not Patroclus in book 12, when he takes inward satisfaction that the Greeks will soon grovel at his feet because of the casualties they have taken; nor Patroclus in book 16 before whom he prays to Zeus, Athena, and Apollo that all the Achaians and all the Trojans perish from the face of the earth.

At this point, Menelaus angrily denounces Antilochus for committing a foul against his horses and unfairly displacing him from the second place in the race he justifiably earned. Here is another potential quarrel which could have gone the way of the dispute between Achilles and Agamemnon in book 1, but the newly emerging graciousness of Achilles appears to be contagious. Antilochus apologizes to Menelaus, who accepts the apology and allows Antilochus to keep the second prize, while accepting the third place prize, a lesser one than he had justifiably earned, for himself. Meriones takes the fourth place prize but now there is one prize for fifth place left unclaimed, a two-handled bowl, as Achilles had produced an additional reward earlier to satisfy the circumstances of Antilochus and Eumelus. What Achilles does with this extra prize is an impressive sign of the way his character is evolving in book 23:

> ...This prize Achilles gave to Nestor and Carrying
> it through the Argive assembly and standing Next

Understanding the Iliad

> to him he said: "Take this, revered elder, and let
> it be a Treasure, a remembrance of the funeral of
> Patroclus; For you will not see him again among the
> Argives; I give you this Prize as a sign of respect,
> for you will no longer fight as a boxer, Nor wrestle,
> nor enter the javelin contest, nor run in a foot race.
> For now old age weighs heavily upon you." Having
> spoken, he put the bowl in Nestor's hands and he
> took it gladly. (23.616-24)

Richardson points out that the Greek word I render as "a sign of respect" (*autōs*, "just like that, i.e. without a contest) is emphatically placed."[38] He emphasizes that Achilles presents this gift because Nestor is no longer able to compete in the sports that take place in the funeral games. That may well have been on Achilles's mind, but I think the real point to stress here is on another phrase in Achilles's address to Nestor: "Old age weighs heavily upon you." Achilles recognizes the common human vulnerability to the debilitating effects of old age. His own fate will be to die before old age takes its toll of him, but in book 24, he is very sensitive to how his aged father, Peleus, is faring. Achilles feels *sorrow* for the inevitable troubles and limitations which old age imposes and his gift is meant to honor Nestor and lift his spirits, which he accomplishes, because Nestor is "glad" when he receives the bowl from Achilles.

With his demonstration of sensitivity to the feelings of Eumelus, Antilochus, and Nestor, we see a new and evolving Achilles emerge in book 23 as he begins to show the capacity to transcend the psychological profile of narcissism: rage in the service of vengeance; insensitivity to the feelings of others, and a grandiose concept of one's power and authority. As the games proceed, Achilles continues to demonstrate humane characteristics that we have not seen before. He intercedes in the wrestling match between Telamonian Ajax and Odysseus when it appears they may injure each other, and declares both to be victors. When Antilochus comes in last after Odysseus and Oïlean Ajax in a foot race and praises the older heroes while complimenting Achilles, Achilles graciously awards him an additional prize for his courtesy. In the combat in full armor between Diomedes and Telamonian Ajax, Achilles implements the consensus of the spectators and halts the contest before Ajax is seriously wounded. As the final

Leon Golden

event of the games, Achilles holds a spear-throwing contest in which Agamemnon and Meriones compete against each other with a cauldron worth an ox as first prize and a spear as second prize. Before the competition can begin, however, Achilles intervenes and says:

> "Son of Atreus, we know how far you are superior to
> all, Greatest in authority and best in spear throwing;
> But do you take this prize back to the hollow ships.
> And let us give the spear to the warrior Meriones,
> if you agree In your heart. For this is what I urge."
> (23.890-94)

In this, the last contest of the games, we observe that humility in his deference to Agamemnon has replaced the grandiosity of his condemnation of the entire Achaian army to disaster as a consequence of the clash with his commander in book 1. Attesting eloquently to the significant transformation in Achilles's character is the fact that, on his own initiative, he performs the conciliatory act of making a gift of an unearned first prize to Agamemnon that brings to striking finality the divisive quarrel that began with Agamemnon stripping Achilles of a prize in book 1.

We must, then, consider the funeral games an event of extreme importance in the *Iliad* for it marks the commencement of Achilles's evolution toward full maturity and ennobled humanity. At play in the character of Achilles in the first twenty-two books of the poem have been murderous rage serving the demands of the *lex talionis,* insensitivity to the feelings of other human beings whether they be friends or foes, and a grandiose conception of his power to control people and events that impact on him without reference to the normative values that dignify human behavior. At play in the character of Achilles in book 23 have been the mastery of his wrath and impulse for vengeance against Agamemnon (although not yet his rage against Hector), his sensitivity to the feelings of others and compassion for those who have lost a race or their youth, and his privileging of humility over grandiosity by sealing his reconciliation with Agamemnon with deference and a prize that he was not obligated to offer. I suggest that this transformation in his character and his transcendence over the destructive forces that characterized his earlier behavior have occurred for the reason that Lowen has given in his discussion of psychological

Understanding the Iliad

types with characteristics similar to those of Achilles: their craving to have someone who needs them over whom they have some form of control and their desperate need *not* to be alone. With the death of Patroclus, Achilles had lost the supportive connection he depends on from at least one other person, but with his sensitive and considerate behavior in the funeral games (think especially of his interaction with Eumelus, Antilochus, and Nestor) he has succeeded in regaining human contact with participants in the games who are bonded to him with respect and gratitude. A far greater challenge awaits him—learning to accommodate himself to mankind's universal inability to remedy or revoke the inevitable tragedies and losses that define the human condition. That crucial lesson, a necessary prerequisite for achieving full maturity in its most humane and civilized form, he will learn from Priam in book 24.

Achilles has put an end to his anger at Agamemnon, but he has not put an end to his rage, longing, sadness, and pain over the death of Patroclus, which is still a fierce provocation for him at the beginning of book 24:

> ...But Achilles wept remembering his friend, nor
> did sleep that Subdues all seize him but he tossed
> and turned, yearning for the Manhood and brave
> strength of Patroclus, and how much he had
> Achieved with him, and the pain he had suffered
> testing his Fortune in wars with men and trouble on
> the sea. (24.3-8)

He can find no way to deal with his complex of painful emotions except by continuous mutilation of Hector's corpse:

> But when he yoked his swift horses beneath His
> chariot, and bound Hector so as to drag him from
> behind, he hauled him three times around the tomb
> of the dead Son of Menoetius. Then he would
> rest again in his hut, but left Patroclus, face down,
> outstretched in the dust (24.14-18)

The gods are aghast at what Achilles has been doing to the body of Hector, and Apollo speaks on their behalf:

Leon Golden

> Achilles has lost all pity and nor does he feel any
> shame
> Shame which harms men greatly but also benefits
> them.
> A person is going to lose someone even dearer,
> Either a brother from the same womb, or a son,
> But when he has wept and mourned, he lets go;
> The Fates have given men an enduring spirit.
> But when Achilles has taken the life of god-like
> Hector,
> He binds him to his team of horses
> And drags him around the tomb of his dear friend.
> This is neither very noble nor very good for him.
> (24.44-52)

Interestingly enough, the words of Apollo closely match the views of the contemporary psychiatrist, Thomas Brady, which I have quoted earlier: "It seems to me that the value we put on revenge...is astonishingly destructive, represents the worst rather than the best of human nature" and, in another passage I have quoted before, "I was once told, and have passed the assertion on to my patients and even friends, that one cannot be called truly civilized until he or she has tamed the talionic impulse, that is, the compulsion to enact the *lex talionis*." In their outrage at Achilles's savage application of the *lex talionis,* the law of revenge, Zeus sends word to Achilles via Thetis that he must allow Priam to ransom Hector's body. We are at a stage here where the principle of double motivation—causation on the divine level that is paired with motivation on the human level for the same event—enters into consideration. The command of the gods at the beginning of book 24 foreshadows subsequent action later in the book as Homer provides insightful and persuasive motivation on the human level for Achilles's profound change of heart toward Hector.

Priam's mission to the Myrmidon camp to offer an immense ransom for the body of Hector is a powerful, transformative experience for Achilles. Priam swiftly enters Achilles's hut and, assuming the posture of a suppliant, pleads with the startled Achilles to grant his request. He reminds Achilles of the similarity between himself and Peleus, who are both on "the doorstep of old age." Peleus, too, may be beset by enemies, but he at least has the comfort of knowing that his brave and powerful son is still alive,

Understanding the Iliad

but Priam has lost forever the one son who could protect him and the city of Troy. And it is for that one son, Hector, that he has come to the Greek ships:

> "In order to free him from you. And I bring
> A countless ransom. But respect the gods, Achilles,
> And pity me, remembering your own father; I am
> More miserable than he. I have endured what no other man
> On earth has ever yet suffered. I have extended my hand
> To the man who killed my son." (24.502-06)

Priam asks Achilles to reflect on the shared destiny between himself and Peleus and of the yet more terrible suffering that he has undergone than that which faces either Peleus or Achilles. In order to provide final, worthy honor to Hector, he has humbled himself in supplication to the man who has both slain his son and mutilated his corpse. Priam's plea:

> ...Roused the desire to weep for his father
> In Achilles; and touching Priam's hand
> He gently moved the old man away.
> Both of them remembered. One of them bewailed
> Man-slaying Hector incessantly as he crouched
> Before Achilles's feet and Achilles wept for his
> Father and then for Patroclus; and their
> Groaning rose through the hut. (24.507-12)

The striking use of the word "gently" to describe Achilles's treatment of Priam signals that we are at a point now of extremely great significance for the evolution of Achilles in the poem. I do not believe that the word "gentle," or a synonym for it, has been used to describe Achilles on any occasion in the epic prior to this point. Up until now, murderous rage without pity characterized Achilles's response to the insult Agamemnon inflicted on him, until it was so quickly and casually nullified by an alliance of convenience in book 19; and up until now, from the death of Patroclus at Hector's hands through the slaughter of twelve Trojan soldiers on his friend's funeral pyre, an even more vicious, murderous rage, without pity, has driven Achilles's actions. Achilles's destructive

Leon Golden

wrath has overwhelmed and delayed the normal emotions of grief we might expect him to feel and demonstrate for Patroclus. Priam's appearance before him, someone who has suffered greatly and has come as a suppliant to Achilles in all humility but without any loss of his human dignity, has, however, dramatically pierced the psychological barriers to an expression of emotion both are now able to participate in that is healing and not destructive. Lowen has something of importance to say about this phenomenon of harmful repression and curative expression of emotion in the clinical, psychiatric context:[39]

> Control is maintained by denying and suppressing
> feeling. Yet the therapeutic endeavor aims at
> helping patients open up and accept their feelings.
> That means that patients must learn to give up
> control. They must learn to let their feelings and
> emotions move them, even allowing themselves
> to be carried away by their emotional responses—
> otherwise they will never know the glory of love and
> the exuberance of joy.

Here for the first time, with Priam as the catalyst, Achilles's wrath—the corrosive, barbaric, and ultimately useless response to his suffering—undergoes a transformation that allows him "to be carried away" by an emotional response, by unrestrained weeping for his father and for Patroclus. He is able, for the first time, to manifest pure sorrow free of vengeance-driven rage. The tears that Achilles sheds penetrate and subvert the impotent façade of invulnerability that has protected his cruel acts of insensitivity to friend and foe alike; Priam's immense suffering has now awakened in Achilles humane pity of a far more profound kind than that he felt for Eumelus's embarrassing failure in the chariot race:

> When god-like Achilles had enough of lament
> And the longing for it had left his heart and limbs,
> Quickly he rose from his chair and raised the old
> man by his hand, pitying his gray head and beard,
> And he addressed him with winged words; "Ah,
> luckless old Man, you have endured much hardship
> in your heart. How did you dare to come alone to
> the ships of the Achaians Into the eyes of the man

Understanding the Iliad

who killed Your many noble sons! Truly your heart
is made of iron. But come, sit on a chair, and let
us nevertheless allow Our grief to lie quietly in our
hearts though we are troubled; No good comes
from cold lamentation; for thus the gods have Spun
destiny so that wretched mortals live in pain while
They are themselves without sorrows" (24.513-26)

Priam's courage represents a heroic code of the human spirit
rather than the battlefield, and in his brave action in coming to
rescue the body of his son and in demonstrating sorrow that
is both unrestrained, and yet expressed with great dignity, he
provides a model of civilized humanity that overcomes Achilles
with pity and tenderness for the grieving father "as his words
enfolded him like wings." Walter Burkert insightfully identified
Priam's perception that the common experience of suffering and
grief has established a kind of human intimacy between himself
and one who had been his ardent enemy. The development of this
intimacy, based on an extremity of suffering, makes possible the
experience of pity which, as Burkert says, is "a bridge between two
persons" who in the relationship between "I and Thou" turn out to
develop a formative unity.[40]

Within the context of this new deeply felt humane experience
of pity that binds him to Priam, Achilles reaches out with words
of consolation that are meant to relieve the old man's pain. He
speaks of the common fate of most of mankind who have as
their destiny lives that contain a mixture of good and evil. Both
his father, Peleus, and Priam have shared this common fate, and
Achilles urges Priam to overcome his grief for Hector because
he will torture himself in vain and still not be able to bring his
son back to life. Priam's newly established intimacy with Achilles
is not strong enough, however, to divert his attention from his
dedication to rescuing the body of his son and giving it the care
and attention it properly deserves. Unwisely using imperatives,
he tells Achilles not to hold him seated in his hut but to release
the body of his son to him and accept in exchange the ransom
he has brought for that purpose. This is a scene of great realism.
Priam's peremptory demand is provocative to Achilles, who is
also still heavily burdened by his grief for Patroclus. In spite of
the admiration and pity he genuinely feels for Priam, he issues a
warning to him not to incite his anger, a warning that represents

Leon Golden

a serious threat to Priam's life and frightens the old man into submission. Thus, Homer persuasively shows that profound loss is not easily overcome and that, despite developing ties between Priam and Achilles based on the recognition of common suffering, beneath the surface for both men remain troubling and angry emotions. The forces, however, that have been at work since book 23 in leading Achilles to healing epiphanies continue their forward momentum. After the momentary flare-up of anger against Priam, Achilles immediately takes control of himself again and the following scene of extreme importance takes place:

> The son of Peleus sprang out of the house like a
> lion, Not alone, but his two warrior companions,
> Automedon and Alcimus, followed whom especially
> Achilles honored Of his comrades since Patroclus
> was dead, and they loosed The horses and mules
> from beneath the yoke and led Inside the old man's
> herald and seated him on a chair; and from The
> strong-wheeled wagon they took the boundless
> ransom For the head of Hector. But they left
> behind two robes and a finely-woven tunic so that
> having covered the body Achilles might give It to
> be carried home. Achilles summoned the Women
> servants and ordered them to wash and Anoint the
> body, carrying it out of sight, so that Priam Might
> not see his son and grieving in his Heart might
> not be able to restrain his wrath when he Caught
> sight of him and thus the heart of Achilles would
> be provoked and he would kill him and transgress
> the commands of Zeus. And when the servants
> had washed the body And anointed it with olive oil,
> they cast about it A beautiful cloak and tunic, and
> Achilles himself Lifted him up and placed him on
> a bier and he and his Comrades raised it onto the
> polished wagon. (24.572-90)

We note a series of acts of compassion, respect, and kindness taking place here: Achilles treats Priam's herald with consideration and gives him a comfortable place to rest inside the hut; he and his men do not claim all of the luxurious ransom given them by Priam, but leave behind three items of fine clothing that will

Understanding the Iliad

be used for covering Hector's body; Achilles orders his female servants to wash Hector's corpse and anoint it, but first to remove it from where Priam might see it and be impelled to express his grief and anger and thus provoke Achilles into killing him; after Hector's body had been washed and anointed, Achilles, *himself,* lifts him up and places him on a pallet; then Achilles and his men together raise the pallet onto Priam's cart. These several acts are all signs of humane feelings of kindness, thoughtfulness, and genuine respect for Priam and Hector, whose body will not be savaged, as Achilles had earlier threatened, by dogs and birds, but will be returned to Troy by his slayer with deference and honor in a royal shroud worthy of a great prince. In this scene, Achilles, linked by a bridge of compassion to Priam, impressively demonstrates an evolving capacity for self-control over the compulsion for revenge that has dominated his behavior earlier. Especially impressive is the fact that, as we have seen, Achilles, *himself,* places Hector's body on a pallet and then together with his friends raises it onto the cart that will bring him home again. Richardson's comments on Achilles's actions here are very much to the point:[41]

> Akhilleus himself supervises the washing, anointing and clothing of the body, and it is he who places it on the bier (589). The same rituals were performed for the body of Patroklos when it was brought back from the battle, at 18.343-53 (washing and anointing, placing on the bier and covering). These preparations would normally be performed by members of the dead man's own family, *and it is highly significant that they should be undertaken by Akhilleus* (italics mine).

From the brutal desecration of Hector's body in books 22 and 23 to serving as the surrogate for his father or a brother in overseeing and directly participating in the preliminary rites for his burial—Achilles has traveled a relatively short span of physical time but an immense distance in terms of emotional and psychological evolution.

The peak of Achilles's gracious magnanimity toward Priam has not yet been reached. Returning to the hut after preparing the body of Hector for the return journey with his father, Achilles announces that appropriate preparations have been made, and

Leon Golden

that early the next morning, Priam will be able to see his son. Once again, Achilles demonstrates compassionate forethought in his treatment of Priam as he acts to secure the ties that have been established between them through the bridge of mutual sympathy that unites two men who have suffered profoundly. Achilles arranges that Priam will see his son and take charge of his body soon, but not immediately, for—as before—there is danger that the old man would not be able to restrain an outburst of grief that could incite Achilles to an act of violence that he knows he must not commit and, in the deepest layers of his being, does not want to commit. Achilles then turns to words of further consolation for Priam by narrating the story of Niobe who had angered Apollo and Artemis by insulting their mother, Leto, for having borne only two children while she herself had given birth to many. In retribution, the children of Leto slew Niobe's twelve children and, although she suffered much from this ordeal, even Niobe remembered in time that she had to eat and so Achilles gently urges Priam that he, too, must also give thought to food and drink. Achilles and his companions then prepare an ample feast of food and wine and Priam partakes of this, his first meal, since the death of his son. After the banquet:

> Then Priam, son of Dardanus, marveled At Achilles, how tall he was and how like one of the gods, And Achilles marveled at Priam, son of Dardanus gazing at His noble appearance and listening to his words. (24.629-82)

This is an awesome moment of intimacy between two men who, united by the common bond of human suffering, have marshaled the inner strength and courage to extinguish the flickering embers of hatred with the ennobling power of admiration and affection.

Now, more than anything else, Priam needs sleep and Achilles orders that a luxurious bed be prepared for him. Then Achilles graciously asks him "How many days do you need for the funeral? I will wait that long and hold back the army" (24.707-08). Priam requests eleven days to honor and bury his son, the hero of Troy, and on the twelfth day, he says, they will be ready to fight again if they must. In all kindness, Achilles grants this truce that will crown Hector's glory with worthy rites of burial. Then Achilles seals his

Understanding the Iliad

promise with an act that again signifies his affection and respect for Priam:

> ...And he took the old man's right hand by the wrist
> So that he might not be afraid in his heart (24.671-2)

There is overwhelming magnanimity in Achilles's words and gesture, and Graham Zanker has accurately described the magnanimity that Achilles ultimately achieves in the *Iliad* as *"unique in its intensity, in its sublimity, and in its centrality in the structure of the poem"* (italics mine).[42]

In the last scene of the last book of the *Iliad,* Achilles's presence, as befits the newly achieved humility that has displaced his earlier grandiosity, is felt only at a distance, in the background, as pride of place is given with great effect to vanquished Hector and we hear the voices of Andromache, Hecuba, and Helen celebrate and lament the fallen hero of Troy. In binding Priam to himself in affection and sympathy, and in the honor and respect he shows to Hector at the climax of the epic, Achilles has achieved a spiritual triumph of momentous proportions: magnanimity, compassion, and humility replace rage, insensitivity, and grandiosity as the forces that drive his actions.

In reaching the point now of making a final, interpretative judgment about the meaning and achievement of the *Iliad,* we might well ponder the words of C.W. MacLeod:[43]

> The *Iliad* is concerned with battle and with men whose life is devoted to winning glory in battle; and it represents with wonder their strength and courage. But its deepest purpose is not to glorify them and still less to glorify war itself. What war represents for Homer is humanity under duress and in the face of death; and so to enjoy or appreciate the *Iliad* is to understand and feel for human suffering.

"Humanity under duress and facing death" in war is one prominent, special case of human suffering, and the *Iliad* recognizes and vividly describes the pain inflicted and sustained in acts of killing and being killed on the battlefield. As MacLeod

Leon Golden

has seen, however, it has not been Homer's intention to limit his concern with suffering to war but to treat it in the much wider sphere where it has general relevance to human existence. Achilles's great anguish in the poem is not caused by wounds he received on the battlefield; the traumatic events that torment him are humiliation at the hands of Agamemnon, which strips him of his human dignity and the slaying of Patroclus by Hector, that makes him aware that his invulnerability is a myth, that there are calamities he is powerless to reverse, and that he is now without the sustaining human contact he desperately needs. The *Iliad's* true greatness derives from the way it probes deeply into the nature of Achilles's suffering as a *human being* rather than as a soldier; it first views his response to humiliation and grief by employing the destructive energy of rage and vengeance so intense and brutal that it approaches the level of a force of nature, as the cosmic struggle between water and fire in book 21 symbolizes, but which is impotent to cure his pain; then it focuses on the healing process by which Achilles is able to renounce his wrath and the impulse for revenge under the guidance of the liberating power of compassion. In this way, the story of the *Iliad* is one which unfolds with escalating relevance to mankind in general for Achilles's evolution in the poem anticipates by three millennia the psychoanalytical view that the ruthless application of the *lex talionis* is a manifestation of barbarism, not civilization, and is doomed to failure.

In the last two books of the *Iliad,* Achilles emerges with a mature comprehension of the reality of the human condition that has greatly tempered his volatile passions and their destructive consequences. Homer did not, however, contemplate the possibility that Achilles could emerge, free and clear, from the dark shadows of his sorrow, from the troubling cognizance of the immense suffering he has experienced and caused, to stifle completely the oppressive forces that have lacerated his soul and so to encounter, in one psychiatrist's view of therapeutic success, "the glory of love and the exuberance of joy." Nevertheless, in his gentle and tender consolation of Priam as a suppliant, in clasping Priam's wrist so he would not be afraid, and in granting a truce of sufficient duration so that unstinting honor can be paid to the slain Hector, Achilles does experience the exaltation of compassionate sympathy for another human being that surely approaches love in

Understanding the Iliad

one of the more elevated and subtle forms it can take in human relationships.

Homer has traced the existence of two heroic codes in the *Iliad*: one, much easier to attain, the heroic code of the battlefield, where killing and being killed brings suffering but also enduring fame; and the other, far more difficult to achieve, the heroic code of the human spirit which gathers its force and vitality from the most profound sources of our humane virtue, from compassion, magnanimity, and humility and, in contrast with the first heroic code, privileges respect for life over the glorification of death. It is with the focus on this second heroic code that Homer, master poet and master analyst of the human condition, chooses, with tragic optimism, to bring the epic story of the *Iliad* to its conclusion.

Chapter 3

The Relationship of the *Iliad* to Greek Tragic Theory and Practice

For Plato, Homer was the "first of the tragic poets" (*Republic* 10.607A) and the "consummate tragic poet" (*Theaetetus* 152E), while for Aristotle it was Homer who initiated and shaped the evolutionary process that reached its climactic fulfillment in the emergence of tragedy as a literary genre (*Poetics* 1448b34-1449a2). While agreeing on Homer's achievement as tragedy's originator and the most influential force behind its evolutionary development, Plato and Aristotle clearly evaluated that status in contradictory ways. Plato's comment recognizes the powerful influence Homer exerted on a literary form for which he felt unrelenting antagonism because of what he judged to be its subversive effects on human character; Aristotle's observation is an admiring recognition of Homer's great achievement in encompassing in his own work the sources of human experience that define the essence of tragedy. Plato's concern is with Homer's potent capacity to evoke unrestrained emotion which leads, in his view, to the subversive tyranny of pleasure and pain over reason in our lives.[1]

Achilles's behavior in the first twenty-two books of the *Iliad* offers a number of examples of expressions of unrestrained emotion that represent the destructive element in tragedy from Plato's point of view. We recall his explosive wrath directed at Agamemnon in book 1, where his rage brings him almost to the

126

Understanding the Iliad

point of murdering his antagonist and then swells to a desire for vengeance against not only Agamemnon, but his entire army. We note his intensely angry rejection in book 9 of the pleas of the embassy that Agamemnon has sent who are his closest friends in the army and how he rejoices in the vision of a totally defeated Achaian army. We watch the outpouring of his vast grief when he learns of Patroclus's death in book 18 and observe him emotionally distraught and on the verge of suicide at that point. And in response to that grief, we witness the berserk and brutal revenge he inflicts on the Trojans in books 20-22, which reaches its climax in the killing of Hector, the inhumane desecration of his corpse, and the sacrifice on Patroclus's funeral pyre of twelve young Trojan soldiers with Achilles savagely slaying them with grim vengeance in his heart. These themes of rage, violence, and revenge have their echo in a number of examples of fifth century Greek tragedy and especially in the plays of Euripides. They repeat themselves throughout the history of world literature and reflect what we might call the oppressive pathos of the human condition. Although Achilles, as we have seen, for twenty-two books of the *Iliad* demonstrates behavior that directly links him to the experience of pathos in tragedy, he significantly reverses direction in the final two books of the poem and causes the dramatic transformation of pathos into the heroic tragedy into which the *Iliad* evolves in the final two books of the epic.

A second major factor governing pathos in Greek tragedy relates to the behavior of the operative power in the universe, the gods. They impose the force of grinding pathos on the lives of human beings in those works in which they act with such amoral cruelty as to deprive mankind of any chance for tragic heroism. We have seen, on the other hand, that while the gods of the *Iliad,* acting out their theological role, are often indifferent to, and even contemptuous of, the human condition, they do *not* foreclose the possibility of tragic heroic behavior for anyone under their sway who chooses to exercise that option.

A prime example in Greek tragedy of a divinity imposing unendurable suffering on human beings is Dionysus in Euripides's *Bacchae* who, without mercy and motivated by the talionic impulse, generates the excruciating pathos that renders human beings totally helpless as a god strips them of all dignity. The action of the *Bacchae* is driven by Dionysus's intention upon his return to Thebes to punish those who have previously denied his

Leon Golden

divinity and to force them to recognize him as a god. The struggle between Dionysus and Thebes, and primarily with its current ruler, Pentheus, is one of cosmic magnitude. E.R. Dodds has accurately and perceptively described the character of the two antagonists and their lethal encounter:[2]

> ...the bestial incarnations reveal Dionysus as something much more significant and much more dangerous than a wine-god. He is the principle of animal life...the hunted and the hunter—the unrestrained potency which man envies in the beasts and seeks to assimilate. His cult was originally an attempt on the part of human beings to achieve communion with this potency. The psychological effect was to liberate the instinctive life in man from the bondage imposed on it by reason and social custom: the worshiper became conscious of a strange new vitality, which he attributed to the god's presence within him...
>
> If Dionysiac worship is an immoral superstition and nothing more, it follows that Pentheus is one of the martyrs of the enlightenment. But it is much easier to blacken Dionysus than to whitewash Pentheus. Some rationalist critics have essayed the latter task; but it takes a resolutely blinkered vision to discover in him 'the defender of the conjugal faith', 'a consistently lovable character'. Euripides could have conceivably have represented him thus; he could certainly have made him a second Hippolytus, fanatical, but with a touching and heroic fanaticism. He has not chosen to do so. Instead he has invested him with the traits of a typical tragedy-tyrant; absence of self-control...willingness to believe the worst on hearsay evidence...or on none...brutality towards the helpless...and a stupid reliance on physical force as a means of settling spiritual problems. In addition he has given him the foolish racial pride of a Hermione...and the sexual curiosity of a Peeping Tom. It is not thus that martyrs of the enlightenment are represented.

Understanding the Iliad

Dodds also perceptively explicates the meaning of the clash that takes place between these two adversaries:[3]

> As the 'moral' of the *Hippolytus* is that sex is a thing about which you cannot afford to make mistakes, so the 'moral' of the *Bacchae* is that we ignore at our peril the demand of the human spirit for Dionysiac experience. For those who do not close their minds against it such experience can be a deep source of spiritual power... But those who repress the demand in themselves or refuse its satisfaction to others transform it by their act into a power of disintegration and destruction, a blind natural force that sweeps away the innocent with the guilty. When that has happened, it is too late to reason or to plead: in man's justice there is room for pity, but there is none in the justice of Nature; to our 'Ought' its sufficient reply is the simple 'Must'; we have no choice but to accept that reply and to endure as we may.

Euripides structures in the *Bacchae* a universe in which there clash antagonistic forces of considerably unequal power which make nonnegotiable demands upon each other. Dodds has focused our attention on the ecstatic nature of Dionysiac worship in which the god demands acts of devotion by his human devotees which unite them to the savage and violent principle of animal life he embodies. The spirit of Dionysiac religion is clearly seen in the nature and force of the climactic act of worship performed by the god's human followers—the tearing apart (*sparagmos*) and eating raw (*omophagia*) of a sacrificial animal. Two vivid, gruesome incidents of *sparagmos* take place in the *Bacchae*. In the first, a messenger describes a group of women, worshipers of Dionysus, whose rites are interrupted by men who wish to profit by arresting them and handing them over to Pentheus, who has vowed to end what he considers to be this dangerous religious frenzy that has swept into his country. We hear from the messenger that the men barely escaped massacre by the women who then turned their attention to the cattle, which were torn to pieces. Even fierce bulls

Leon Golden

were hurled to the ground and rapidly stripped of their flesh by the maddened Bacchae (735-47).

In the second incident, we find Pentheus maliciously and vengefully guided by Dionysus to spy on the rites employed by the Bacchants to worship their god. There, the mother of Pentheus, Agave, has been driven into a state of maddened religious ecstasy so that she can serve as Dionysus's mechanism for imposing an unbelievably cruel and severe punishment on Pentheus. When she catches sight of her son observing the Bacchants in their ecstatic rites, Dionysus makes her see him in the form of a wild animal, a mountain lion, an apparition that stirs her in a mad fury to mobilize her troop of women to capture and kill the intruding beast. Dionysus dedicates himself joyfully to the task of aiding the women in pursuit of revenge by bending a tall tree to the ground, carefully placing Pentheus on the tip of it, cautiously allowing the tree to spring back into position without unseating Pentheus and then summoning the women to take vengeance on their persecutor. The *sparagmos* of a son at the hands of his mother and her allies involves the tearing of his limbs from his body, the macabre activity of rolling pieces of his flesh into a ball and playing a game of catch with it, and impaling his severed head on a thyrsus (1122-43).

In the aftermath of this brutal human sacrifice to the god, Pentheus's grandfather, Cadmus, having assembled the shredded remnants of Pentheus's body, confronts Dionysus who— unsatisfied with the disaster already accomplished to Cadmus's family—pronounces further harsh penalties on the much-suffering old man for his earlier failure to acknowledge his divinity. In vain, Pentheus pleads with the god as follows:

> *Cadmus*
> We beseech you, Dionysus, We have wronged you.
>
> *Dionysus*
> You have learned too late, when it was necessary,
> you did not know what you needed to know.
>
> *Cadmus*
> We have learned this; but your punishment goes
> too far.

Understanding the Iliad

Dionysus
For I was mocked by you although I am a god.

Cadmus
When it comes to rage, gods should not imitate
mortals.

Dionysus
Long ago my father Zeus approved this. (1344-49)

We see here the large difference between the divine/human
relationship in the *Iliad* and the same relationship in dramas of
pathos like the *Bacchae*. In the *Iliad,* the gods do not rescue men
from death and destruction, even those who have been dearest to
them for mortals are, ultimately, trivial entities in the divine order
of the universe, as we know from Zeus's scornful view of human
insignificance (17.446-47). Yet in the *Iliad,* gods do not stand in
the way of human beings living and dying by a heroic code that
confers dignity upon themselves, however insignificant they may
be in the larger scheme of things. In many tragedies of pathos,
such as the *Bacchae,* the forces that control the world—the
gods—make the demonstration of tragic heroism completely
impossible, and in its place provide only a human destiny filled
with humiliation, degradation, and absurdity.

Nowhere in the *Iliad* does a divinity strip a human being of
his or her humanity with the kind of sardonic joy which motivates
Dionysus in his pursuit of revenge against Pentheus. There
are three important occasions when we observe this merciless
vendetta against a fallible mortal. The first occurs at 616-41, where
the god describes how, in the manger where Pentheus attempted
to imprison him, he created an image of a bull which Pentheus
futilely sought to rope as sweat poured from his body and he bit
his lips in fury. The god relates how he quietly sat by observing
the fiasco and then proceeded to set the palace on fire. Pentheus,
anxiously commanding the servants to bring water to extinguish
the blaze, rushed into the building thinking that Dionysus might
have escaped. There he only found another image made of
insubstantial air, which he foolishly and ineffectively kept stabbing,
thinking it to be Dionysus. Dionysus's humiliation of Pentheus in
this scene ends with the actual burning down of the palace itself

Leon Golden

and with the mocking condemnation of his antagonist as a mere man who dared to enter into combat with a god.

The second scene of cruel humiliation occurs at 810-977, where Dionysus convinces Pentheus to adopt the dress and behavior of the Bacchants so that he may have a chance to see them performing their rites. The god transforms Pentheus into a Bacchic worshiper who is anxious about whether he is wearing his female attire and carrying the thyrsus correctly. Before Dionysus sends him off to undergo his humiliating transformation, he says in an aside that it his intention to make him into a laughingstock among the Thebans as he is led through the city in female attire. He triumphantly looks forward to the slaughter of Pentheus at the hands of his mother, and evokes the ominous mystery of his own divinity when he identifies himself, Dionysus, as a god who is "most terrible and most gentle to mankind" (860-61). The final words exchanged between the god and the man in this scene are most terrifying, for they are filled with cynical, cryptic remarks of Dionysus that evade the comprehension of Pentheus (966-70). As Dodds perceptively notes at this point, "the Stranger makes ambiguous promises which Pentheus, excited beyond control by the prospect of his triumphant return, continually interrupts."[4] The troubling ambiguities actually begin three lines before this passage, where Dionysus says to Pentheus, in Dodds's translation (note, *ad loc.,* 963-65), "you bear the burden for the state" which to P[entheus] means "you toil on its behalf" but to the audience "you suffer for its offences." At 965-66, we hear the bitterly ironic promise by Dionysus that he will be Pentheus's "protecting escort" in guiding him to the Bacchants, but that someone else will lead him back. Pentheus immediately imagines that Dionysus is referring to his mother, who will honor him for his courageous actions in this way and has no inkling of the disastrous fate that will befall him at her hands. When Dionysus responds with ominous ambiguity at 967 that Pentheus will be a remarkable sight on his return journey, he innocently and pathetically replies that "it is for this purpose that I go." After translating 968 as "you shall ride home," Dodds perceptively comments that "Pentheus, picturing himself in a chariot or litter at the head of a train of captives protests coyly: 'You propose to pamper me.'" Dodds reinforces for us Pentheus's expectation of luxurious treatment for foiling the Bacchic rites of the women with the bitterly ironic comment, since his mother will be carrying his severed head, that he will

Understanding the Iliad

return "in [his] mother's embrace." Dodds translates the final words exchanged between the two adversaries as follows:

Pentheus
You are determined actually to spoil me.

Dionysus
To spoil you, —yes in my fashion.

Pentheus
I go to claim my due.

On this assertion by Pentheus, Dodds comments: "It is his last word, unconsciously significant, and the audience shudders."

We have already discussed the third, climactic humiliation imposed on Pentheus by Dionysus when, after Pentheus places himself in Dionysus's "protective" hands, the god leads him into the clutches of Agave and the band of maddened Bacchants to be slaughtered and torn apart, a human sacrifice in the religious rite of *sparagmos* for the god, Dionysus.

The literature of pathetic tragedy, when it does not depend on divine malice, focuses on human cruelty and depravity as the instruments for defining the human condition. In Greek tragedy, the most extreme manifestations of pathos are found in the work of Euripides and no more cruel demonstration of its oppressive force in the service of the talionic principle can be found than in the *Medea*. In this play, we have a depiction of the betrayal of Medea by Jason, her frenzied indignation in response to Jason's plans to abandon her, and the terrible retribution she takes in requital of the injury she has suffered. From the chorus and nurse we learn early in the play that Medea does not accept her situation in a "civilized" way as some routine circumstance often experienced in marriages but, rather, reacts with the dangerous and threatening fury that has its source in her non-Greek, "barbaric" origins. Creon, the tyrant of Thebes and father of Jason's intended new bride, intuits the great danger his family faces from Medea and decides upon her immediate banishment. Medea, however, skillfully thwarts his plan and obtains a reprieve of sufficient time to arrange the safe haven she will need for herself after conducting the orgy

Leon Golden

of slaughter that alone will satisfy her thirst for vengeance. In a heated exchange with Jason, she enumerates the sacrifices she has made for his sake which have totally alienated her from her family and native land, and she is outraged when he cavalierly dismisses her services to him by attributing only a modest value to them—although they included his acquisition of the Golden Fleece. He sophistically informs her that she has been vastly overcompensated for any help she has given him by her "good fortune" in being brought to Greece, a civilized nation, he argues, with advanced laws where she has had the opportunity to become famous. When he goes so far as to suggest that he is prepared now to demonstrate that his marriage with Creon's daughter is actually in Medea's best interest, her fury explodes.

After securing a place of refuge from Aegeus, king of Athens, Medea is ready to put her plan for vengeance into action, a plan that involves a pretended reconciliation with Jason and his new wife by sending her two sons to the intended bride with a gift of clothing corrupted by poison that will cause most painful death. After her gifts are received and work their terrible effect, Medea is aware that the next horrifying step she will have to take will be the killing of her own children. Her plan involves stripping Jason of any hope of children from his new wife, who will soon be dead, and any hope of future support from their own children, whose lives she will presently extinguish. When the chorus argues that she must not commit the horrific act of killing the innocent children, she responds that she *will* carry out the savage deed, because in this way she can hurt Jason the most. After the children have delivered the instruments of death to Creon's daughter, their fate is sealed, for she must kill them before Creon does and she must make Jason feel the pain of their death. Although the thought of killing her children fills Medea with anguish, the desire for vengeance, the talionic impulse, is a greater force in her psyche. At 1078-80 she says:

> I understand the horror of the deed I am going to
> do but my wrath is stronger than sound judgment—
> wrath which is the cause of the greatest disasters
> for mortals.

After news of the cruel deaths suffered by Jason's wife and her father is brought to Medea, she carries out the murder of

Understanding the Iliad

her children. When Jason appears on the scene to confront her for her outrageous crimes, she taunts him with the triumphant way in which she has made her enemies suffer. She finds joyful satisfaction in the pain she has inflicted on Jason, even at the cost of her children's lives, a crime that her conscience can tolerate as long as Jason suffers excruciating torment. When Jason warns her that she too will be a partner in suffering for the slaughtered children, she responds that she considers her pain profitable as long as he cannot mock her (1362). The bitter debate between the two of them reaches its climax at lines 1393-98:

> Ja. You loathsome abomination, you child-killer
> Me. Go home and bury your wife!
> Ja. I go having lost my two sons.
> Me. Don't grieve yet; wait until old age.
> Ja. My children, so very dear to me.
> Me. Dear to their mother, not to you.
> Ja. And yet you killed them?
> Me. Yes, in order to plunge you into misery.

In this play, Jason's treatment of Medea is characterized by ingratitude and callous exploitation in the service of the most important motivations in his life—ambition and greed. Although Medea commits herself totally to him, he cavalierly abandons her and dismisses the value of her services as he sees an opportunity to achieve social and political gain for himself. He has no idea that his humiliation of her will trigger an overwhelmingly violent act of revenge when she privileges her hatred for the one who has abused her over her love for her own children. Human beings corrupted by ambition, greed, and the talionic principle and gods totally merciless in their dealings with human beings are the stuff out of which pathos and pathetic tragedy are created. This is the kind of tragedy which has earned Plato's condemnation as a subversion of the human spirit, but it remains a dominant aspect of tragic drama from his day to ours.

Aristotle also observed the prominence of pathos but he focused his attention on a very different kind of tragedy in establishing his famous and influential definition of tragedy. I want to show now that the *Iliad* serves as the source, either directly or indirectly, also of this other form of tragedy which affirms the existence of validating nobility within the context of great human

Leon Golden

suffering, in opposition to the depiction of utter degradation and depravity that characterize the many works of pathos that dominate the tragic genre. In pursuing this goal, I will want to develop the argument that it is the *Iliad* in its representation, not of the pathos which characterizes much of the epic, but its celebration of the *tragic heroism* which Achilles ultimately achieves, that provides the basis, consciously or subconsciously, for the theory of tragedy Aristotle develops in the *Poetics,* a theory that is far more profound, subtle, and complex than the simplistic Platonic identification of tragedy with degrading pathos.

First, we need to review the essential characteristics of the tragic heroism of Achilles in the *Iliad.* It is clear, I believe, that if the *Iliad* had ended with book 22, we would have a work of pathos, pure and simple, of the kind which Plato protested against with great vehemence. For twenty-two books of the poem, Achilles, we have seen, is driven by narcissistic wrath in his interaction with other human beings. His dispute with Agamemnon in book 1 leads him not only to murderous intentions against his commander, but to an all-encompassing contempt for the entire Achaian army, including those he loves the most in that army, and a desire to see the entire Achaian host suffer devastating punishment for its failure to rise up in support of him in his dispute with Agamemnon. After abandoning his own former allies to what he hopes will be a punishing defeat, we see Achilles returning to the war only after his best friend, Patroclus, is killed in battle by Hector, and then we find him pursuing a savage, inhumane vengeance against the Trojans which reaches its climax in the barbaric mutilation of Hector's corpse. His viciousness at this point differs little in its malicious intent from the violence committed by Medea against her enemies. It also bears a relationship in its intensity, although it does not equal in magnitude, the savage persecution waged by the god Dionysus against Pentheus.

It is what happens in the *Iliad* and to Achilles in books 23 and 24 that extends the boundaries of tragedy beyond pathos to the level of tragic heroism. The I/Thou encounter between Achilles and Priam works a powerful transformation in Achilles's view of himself and his relationship to other human beings. His aspiration for extreme revenge to pay for the excruciating pain he has experienced, first as a direct result of Agamemnon's contemptuous insults, and then from the sorrow that overwhelms him after Patroclus is slain by Hector, gradually relaxes its hold

Understanding the Iliad

over him as he experiences the wondrous humanity and true heroism of the father of his hated enemy who has suffered even more pain than he has. He arrives at an epiphany, a moment of clarification about the nature of the human condition, that allows him to bring to the surface of his consciousness capacities for humane interaction with others, friends and foes alike, that have been absent throughout the earlier events of the *Iliad*. The fierce and destructive narcissism that has subverted his dignity and character, greatly disturbing our evaluation of him, gives way to compassionate actions that now elevate him greatly in our estimation.

Because of this significant change in his world view, the poem undergoes its own transformation in its final two books, from a work of pathos to one of impressive tragic heroism. The concept of tragic heroism as it unfolds in the *Iliad* is of great importance because Aristotle's influential concept of tragedy as presented in the *Poetics* can only apply to this dimension of the genre and *not* to that broad range of works characterized by the pathos that Plato, for one, has singled out as determinative for the expression of tragedy. In consciously or subconsciously following the guidance of the *Iliad* when developing the view of ideal tragedy that is embedded in his discussion of the genre in the *Poetics,* Aristotle validates the decisive role he has attributed to Homer in shaping the evolution of tragedy as a literary genre. To demonstrate the important connection that I see existing between Homer, Aristotle, and fifth century tragic drama, I will need to bring into focus the key elements of Aristotle's discussion of tragedy as they apply both to the *Iliad* and to the fifth century drama that Aristotle clearly uses as a paradigm for his analysis of tragedy and which also is a work characterized by tragic heroism, the *Oedipus Rex* of Sophocles.

Essential to Aristotle's view of ideal tragedy are two factors: (1) that it represents events, experiences, emotions, and characters that are evocative of *pity and fear* and (2) that these pitiful and fearful circumstances represented and aroused in tragedy undergo a process known as *catharsis*. Aristotle makes explicit the necessary conditions that must be present for pity and fear to exist in tragedy:[5]

> Nor should an excessively evil person fall from
> good fortune into bad fortune for although such

Leon Golden

a plot would be in accordance with our human sympathy, it would be neither pitiable nor fearful since the former is concerned with the person who undeservedly falls into misfortune and the latter is concerned with the person who is like ourselves, pity [as I say] relating to the one who is undeservedly unfortunate and fear to the one who is like ourselves so that what turns out [in such a plot] would be neither pitiable nor fearful. What remains [as the appropriate hero for the ideal tragedy manifesting pity and fear] is a person whose character lies in between extreme virtue and extreme evil. This is such a person who is neither exceptional in virtue and justice nor one who falls into misfortune through vice and depravity but on account of some *hamartia* (error, mistake, miscalculation) of those who enjoy great reputation and prosperity, for example, Oedipus and Thyestes and illustrious persons from such families. It is necessary then for the plot that is to turn out well to have a single rather than double outcome, as some say, and to change not to good fortune from bad fortune but the opposite, from good fortune to bad fortune, and not because of depravity but because of a great *hamartia* (error, mistake, miscalculation) either on the part of such a person as has been described [one like ourselves] or of a better rather than a worse one.

It has long been recognized that Sophocles's *Oedipus Rex* provides the outstanding example of a tragic hero whose fate evokes from an audience the emotions of pity and fear. The tragic circumstances of Oedipus are well known: when he is informed by an oracle that he is to kill his father and live in incest with his mother, he flees the city in which he is living in order to avoid these horrible crimes. It is his fate, however, in spite of all of his precautions, to commit those very crimes he urgently attempted to avoid, and for the responsibility to fall on him to discover the true identity of his father's murderer. This he does even when it becomes clear that his investigation is leading directly to himself as the inadvertent slayer of his father. The key points that we must

Understanding the Iliad

remember about Oedipus is that his humanity rebelled against an oracle that doomed him to unspeakable crimes and that he chose the suffering involved in abandoning hearth and home rather than to submit to this great catastrophe. Then, when warned that he was on the verge of discovering information that could destroy him, he did not turn aside from the search for a truth that alone could emancipate his city from the plague that was ravaging it. Rather, he pressed on, regardless of personal consequences, to obtain a revelation that overwhelmed him with pain and sorrow.

Oedipus is clearly a model for the character Aristotle requires as the hero of an ideal tragedy, someone as good or better than we are who falls from happiness to misery because of some *hamartia* (error, mistake, miscalculation) and evokes from us the emotions of *pity and fear*. E.R. Dodds has given us an extremely perceptive analysis of Oedipus's character as an ideal Aristotelian tragic hero:[6]

> To ask about a character in fiction "Was he a good man?" is to ask a strictly meaningless question: Since Oedipus never lived we can answer neither "Yes" nor "No." The legitimate question is "Did Sophocles intend us to think of Oedipus as a good man?" This *can* be answered—not by applying some ethical yardstick of our own, but by looking at what the characters in the play say about him. And by that test the answer is "Yes." In the eyes of the Priest in the opening scene he is the greatest and noblest of men, the saviour of Thebes who with divine aid rescued the city from the Sphinx. The Chorus has the same view of him: he has proved his wisdom, he is the darling of the city, and never will they believe ill of him (504ff.). And when the catastrophe comes, no one turns round and remarks, "Well, but it was your own fault: it must have been; Aristotle says so."
>
> In any case I cannot understand Sir Maurice Bowra's idea that the gods *force* on Oedipus the knowledge of what he has done. They do nothing of the kind; on the contrary, what fascinates us is the spectacle of a man freely choosing, from the

Leon Golden

> highest motives, a series of actions which lead to his own ruin. Oedipus might have left the plague to take its course; but pity for the sufferings of his people compelled him to consult Delphi. When Apollo's word came back, he might still have left the murder of Laius uninvestigated; but piety and justice required him to act. He need not have forced the truth from the reluctant Theban herdsman; but because he cannot rest content with a lie, he must tear away the last veil from the illusion in which he has lived so long. Teiresias, Jocasta, the herdsman, each in turn tries to stop him, but in vain; he must read the last riddle, the riddle of his own life. The immediate cause of Oedipus' ruin is not "fate" or "the gods"—no oracle said that he must discover the truth—and still less does it lie in his own weakness; what causes his ruin is his own strength and courage, his loyalty to Thebes, and his loyalty to the truth. In all this we are to see him as a free agent; hence the suppression of the hereditary curse. And his self-mutilation and self-banishment are equally free acts of choice.

The evidence, as Dodds has presented it, for Oedipus's character as being as good or better than our own is most persuasive. Aristotle, however, insisted that the tragic hero, in order to evoke the emotions of pity and fear, must exhibit a *hamartia* (error, mistake, miscalculation) that makes credible his fall from good fortune to bad fortune without involving him in moral degradation. Dodds has not uncovered such a *hamartia* for Oedipus's "strength and courage," which he certainly possesses, cannot be an error, mistake, or miscalculation and if those virtues were not accompanied by a *hamartia,* then we would have the spectacle of a completely virtuous person suffering the fall from happiness to misery which Aristotle calls "repellent" and rejects as a pattern for tragedy. I think, however, that we can locate a special kind of *hamartia* within Oedipus that does not subvert his undisputed moral virtue and strength of character. When Oedipus sought the aid of the oracle at Delphi in discovering the identity of his parents, we recall that the response he received ignored his question but, instead, predicted that he would commit patricide

Understanding the Iliad

and incest. In a reaction to that oracle with which we must all sympathize, Oedipus rebelled against submitting to the crimes it ordained and fled from the city where his putative parents were living, so that he would never find himself in circumstances where the dread oracle could be fulfilled. Although Oedipus assumed that he understood the oracle and how he needed to deal with it, he was totally unable to penetrate into its true meaning and into the will and intention of the god, Apollo, for whom the oracle spoke.

Thus, Oedipus manifests the most fundamental and universal human *hamartia* possible—the profound limitation of the human intellect in fathoming the mystery of divine will and purpose, which gives rise to the consequent errors, mistakes, and miscalculations that flow from this flawed perception of reality. This is an intellectual *hamartia* that is totally free of any moral stigma but it nevertheless leads to disaster. The story of Oedipus thus provides us with the ideal paradigm for a drama of tragic heroism: the depiction of someone as good or better than we are who commits a great intellectual error that is completely free of moral pollution and is, on the contrary, performed in the service of high moral purpose but leads to a fall from happiness to misery. Such a circumstance engenders pity for the undeserved misfortune of a character whose motive for action was purely virtuous and moral, but who was placed in an impossible situation by a divine force too powerful for him to master. Here, too, since we recognize in Oedipus someone as good or better than ourselves, we must experience fear, in Aristotle's terms, for our own powerlessness to avoid the horrific consequences that befall Oedipus.

Oedipus's tragic heroism is a constant throughout Sophocles's play, while Achilles's tragic heroism emerges only at the end of the *Iliad*. Nevertheless, that tragic heroism, I argue, has a similar potency, as in the case of Oedipus to evoke the Aristotelian emotions of pity and fear. Oedipus exerted every effort humanly possible to avoid committing the crimes he was fated to accomplish, and which the god permitted to happen, and so it is easy to experience pity and fear for him. Achilles must take full responsibility for the suffering and death he caused to happen in the first twenty-two books of the *Iliad*. Thus, it is easy to take an unforgiving attitude toward him for much of the poem. Yet the great reversal in his behavior in books 23 and 24, where he emerges from the abyss of human degradation to operate on a plane of existence where he manifests the deepest human compassion

Leon Golden

toward his former enemies, should have a profound effect on our attitude toward him. His encounter with the heroic suffering and endurance of Priam brings about an epiphany concerning the nature of human existence that sweeps away the destructive narcissism, the *hamartia,* that has motivated his actions for so long and permits a heretofore hidden magnanimity to surface.

In Achilles, we see a human being whose narcissistic vision of the world had led him with cruel indifference to inflict much suffering on friends and foes alike, but who has the moral capacity to undergo a redemptive transformation of his character. His merciless desecration of the corpse of Hector does nothing to ameliorate his pain, but the spectacle of Priam's noble, brave, and compassionate grieving for the son Achilles had massacred has a powerful and illuminating effect on him. When he touches the wrist of Priam so that he will not have any fear, when he bestows careful and considerate treatment on Hector's body and grants a magnificent funeral for him both out of respect for Priam, for whom he now feels great admiration, and to honor a noble adversary, we are led to make a major reevaluation of him. To feel pity for Achilles, we must put emphasis on his eventual redemption as a human being, not on the total innocence of his behavior as in the case of Oedipus. Our view of how deserved or undeserved his suffering is undergoes modification and change as we reflect on his emerging capacity for humane compassion and we become convinced that he possesses an impressive dimension of moral virtue that has only lately freed itself for expression from its narcissistic prison.

Homer skillfully leads us to the understanding that the acts of savagery and cruel indifference committed by Achilles are not the product of a sadistic and evil temperament but the result of psychological demons that require exorcism. Many will recognize in themselves, and therefore fear, a vulnerability to mistakes, errors, or miscalculations of varying severity that may have or have had serious consequences, but if they also aspire to a reversal of the behavior that led to those consequences, then they will be able to admire in Achilles—who actually achieved this kind of ultimate triumph over himself—someone they believe to be like themselves or better than they are, and thus pity him in his encounter with misery and suffering.

It is not difficult to present arguments relating to Achilles's ability to generate pity and fear in an audience. The question

Understanding the Iliad

of catharsis in the *Iliad* and Greek tragedy is a much more complicated one because no final resolution has been achieved which is universally accepted as to what Aristotle actually meant by this term. The traditional interpretation of catharsis as a process analogous to medical purgation has been widely influential since Jakob Bernays advocated it in the middle of the nineteenth century. This interpretation is based on the appearance of the term "catharsis" in a passage in Aristotle's *Politics* in which it describes the process of curing certain excited emotional states by the use of ecstatic musical melodies that serve as a homeopathic purging and cure of those states. It is Bernays's thesis, and that of those who hold the purgation theory of catharsis, that pity and fear which Aristotle identified as the essential experiences of tragedy must be considered as negative and oppressive emotional experiences that, like physical illness, are in need of purgation and cure. There are, however, very strong reasons for *not* identifying the process described by catharsis in the passage from the *Politics*[7] with the function of catharsis in the *Poetics*. Aristotle alerts us to the fact there is a significant difference between his use of the term in the two treatises when he specifically states in the *Politics* passage that he is using it only generally in this context but that he will speak more clearly about it in the *Poetics*. I maintain that he has accomplished this promise, not admittedly by offering a definition of catharsis, but just as effectively by asserting that the pleasure and goal of all artistic mimesis is the cognitive one of *learning and inference*: Gerald Else has offered what I believe to be an irrefutable argument for maintaining a sharp distinction between the signification of the term catharsis in the very different contexts of the *Politics* and the *Poetics*:[8]

> And there is another objection to Bernays' interpretation, which would have long since been recognized as fatal if the authority of the *Politics* passage had not been accepted as beyond dispute. His interpretation, no matter how adapted or refined, is inherently and indefeasibly *therapeutic*. It presupposes that we come to tragic drama (unconsciously, if you will) as patients to be cured, relieved, restored to psychic health. But there is not a word to support this in the *Poetics,* not a hint that the end of the drama is to cure or alleviate

Leon Golden

pathological states. On the contrary it is evident in every line of the work that Aristotle is presupposing *normal* auditors, normal states of mind and feeling, normal emotional and aesthetic experience.

The following passage in the *Poetics* indicates that Aristotle is applying his remarks about tragedy in general and catharsis in particular in that treatise to a normal audience and not one in need of medical or psychiatric therapy:[9]

Two causes appear to have brought poetry into existence and these are natural causes. For the process of *mimesis* is natural to mankind from childhood on and it is in this way that human beings differ from other animals, because they are the most imitative of them and achieve their first learning experiences through *mimesis,* and all human beings receive pleasure through *mimesis.* A proof of this is what happens in reality; for there are some things which are painful to us when we see them in reality, but we take pleasure in viewing the most precise representations of them, for example, the most despised wild animals and corpses. The reason for this is that the act of learning is not only most pleasant to philosophers but, in a similar way, to everyone else, only others share in this pleasure to a more limited degree. For it is on account of this that we take pleasure when we see representations, because it turns out in our viewing of them we learn and infer what each thing is, for example that this is that.

Aristotle is quite explicit in this passage as to the goal, pleasure, and purpose of all works of art. They are a fundamental means by which human beings come to learn about reality and their essential pleasure is a cognitive one, providing the intellectual pleasure which is an essential characteristic for all normal human beings. Thus catharsis in the *Poetics* as a central feature of Aristotle's definition of tragedy must have an application to the broadest possible audience in full possession of those intellectual faculties which facilitate the process and pleasure of *learning and*

Understanding the Iliad

inference. We must then reject, as Else has argued, explanations of catharsis in the *Poetics* related to medical purgation in the literal sense in which it has been interpreted as well as other theories that fail to accommodate the cognitive, intellectual dimension of the concept which is required by the passage from the *Poetics* I have cited above. There is, however, good reason to believe that Aristotle meant by catharsis in the *Poetics* the process we can identify as *intellectual clarification* and I wish now to review the evidence and arguments for this interpretation.

We start by recognizing that *catharsis,* in addition to its other meanings, does and can mean *intellectual clarification* in Greek since it is used by Epicurus, Philodemus, and Plato to convey the sense of clarification, explanation, and the process of removing ignorance from the mind of human beings by verbal means. Moreover, it is this sense, *and only this sense,* that is consistent with Aristotle's identification, cited above, of *learning and inference* as the essential pleasure found by audiences in all forms of artistic mimesis. Further, it is this sense, *and only this sense,* that is consistent with Aristotle's statement at *Poetics* 1451b5-7 that *"Poetry therefore is more philosophical and more significant than history, for poetry deals more with the universal and history more with the particular."* The apprehension of the universal, which is achieved by the process of *learning and inference* has nothing whatsoever to do with the purgation of physical or mental illness and everything to do with our cognitive faculties. We have then seen that catharsis bears the signification of "intellectual clarification" in Greek (as well as other meanings), that it has far more relevance than "purgation" to Aristotle's explicit recognition of the pleasure and purpose of poetry as a process of learning and inference, and that far more than "purgation" it has a direct relationship to Aristotle's identification of the philosophical dimension of poetry.

Further strong evidence for the interpretation of catharsis as *intellectual clarification* is found in Aristotle's discussion of the structure of the plot in tragedy with its characteristics of lucidity and persuasiveness that necessarily require for their apprehension an act of *intellectual clarification* and not one of *medical purgation.* In his discussion of plot, Aristotle asserts that a tragedy must be an imitation of a "complete and whole action having a proper magnitude," that it must have a beginning, middle, and end that have necessary and appropriate connections with each other,

145

Leon Golden

and that the plot should unfold "through a series of incidents that are in accordance with probability or necessity."[10] In addition, he states that the action of a tragedy must be structured "in such a way that if any one part is transposed or removed, the whole will be disordered and disunified."[11] These essential requirements for plot relate to the coherence of the structure of a work of art and to the logical and psychological persuasiveness of its action for an audience—characteristics that play a critical role in enabling the process of *learning and inference* to take place.

On the issue of what happens to human beings in their encounters with tragic literature, and thus with the process of catharsis, another authoritative voice should be heard. This is the astute and observant voice of the psychiatrist and classicist, Bennett Simon:[12]

> Pity and terror are not purged, but transmuted and integrated into a new level of response and understanding. In this respect, I believe that Aristotle's notion of catharsis has been misunderstood to mean a primitive kind of purging. The Oedipus plays of Sophocles illustrate the movement from primitive dread of pollution because of unspeakable deeds to a more refined and focused sense of moral responsibility. Terror and madness are not made to disappear; they are refined and integrated in the dramatic resolutions.
>
> Related to the changes in the experience of emotions is a reshuffling and reintegration of thoughts and emotions. "Tragic knowledge" implies that by the end of the play the characters and the audience know things they did not know before, and know them in a way they have not experienced before. If we consider Aristotle's notion of the pleasure that tragedy provides, we find that a scale of pleasures is implied. The pleasure of tragedy is of a higher order than the more undifferentiated desires and lusts of humankind. Tragedy, too, must in some ways stir up the body as well as the soul; but Aristotle's views of the highest forms of pleasure, including that of tragedy, assume an increasing differentiation of the bodily appetites and

Understanding the Iliad

responses along with more discriminating cognitive responses....

Finally, tragedy should bring some altered and new sense of what one is and who he is in relation to those around him. The tragic figures in the play struggle with their relationships and obligations to those in their past, present, and future. The audience acquires a new sense of the possibilities in being human and in coming to terms with the forces that are more powerful than any one individual.

The plot of the *Oedipus Rex* is a powerful example of how the act of *learning, inference, and intellectual clarification* unfolds in a drama. We must observe the course of action Oedipus followed in doing what he could, what any mortal could do, to avoid the moral catastrophe that descends upon him, and we must note how the limitations inherent in the human condition triggered intellectual errors that brought about his tragic destiny. We are drawn into the unfolding plot of this play *intellectually* as well as emotionally as we try to understand the character, actions, and fate of Oedipus and this becomes a process of *learning and inference* about human behavior and the human condition. The plot of the drama does not have as its primary purpose the stripping or purging from us the emotions of pity and fear but, rather, the goal of leading us to *understand*, deeply and fully, the role of these experiences in defining the theme of *tragic heroism* that emerges when human beings are forced to grapple with circumstances well beyond their control.

It is my contention that the *Iliad* provides the model for the view of catharsis as intellectual clarification which I believe is at the core of Aristotle's theory of tragedy and manifests itself in the *Oedipus Rex*. We have seen that the action of the *Iliad* begins with the quarrel between Achilles and Agamemnon in book 1, a quarrel that evokes from Achilles's manifestations of murderous rage directed first at Agamemnon and the Achaian army and then at Hector and the Trojan forces. We noted Achilles's ambition to wreak vengeance on Agamemnon by inflicting death and destruction on the entire Achaian army. We recall his rejection in book 9 of the entreaties of his best friends in the Achaian army to come to their aid and ward off sure death that threatens them.

Leon Golden

We remember how coldly he rejects these appeals and how warmly he anticipates the destruction of his own army because of the pain that had been inflicted on him by Agamemnon. We described Achilles's behavior in books 1 and 9 and in the violent campaign he wages against the Trojans on his return to battle in book 20, culminating in his brutal slaying of Hector in book 22, as a significant distortion of normal human behavior. We cited the principal characteristics of that distortion—murderous rage, insensitivity, and grandiosity—as characteristics of a pattern of behavior identified in psychoanalytical terms as *narcissism*. Through book 22, I have argued, Achilles's actions in the epic are driven by these narcissistic forces. If the *Iliad* had ended at this point, then it would have been the epic model for tragedies of pure pathos of the kind that permeates the dramas of Euripides. In books 23 and 24, however, the Aristotelian processes of recognition (*anagnorisis*) and reversal (*peripeteia*) are at work in Achilles's psyche in such a way as to transform the epic from pathos to *heroic tragedy*.

Our argument has shown that recognition for Achilles is a much more subtle psychological enterprise than Oedipus's identification of himself as the killer of Laius, his real father, and the son and husband of Jocasta, his real mother. With the death of Patroclus and its aftermath, Achilles comes to recognize important facts about himself, beginning with an understanding of the true insignificance and folly of his blind rage against Agamemnon and the Achaian army and his uncontrollable wrath against the Trojans and, especially, Hector, the killer of Patroclus. He learns the bitter lesson that his brutal slaughter and desecration of the body of Hector offers neither satisfaction nor solace for his anger and grief, and he perceives how unsatisfactory and futile has been his narcissistic commitment, insensitive, grandiose, and murderous, to vengeance as a motivating force in his life. With the death of Patroclus, as we have seen, Achilles is left alone and isolated from significant human contacts. We have argued that, recognizing his profound isolation, Achilles instituted the funeral games for Patroclus in book 23, which provided him once again access to the community of the Achaian army. These recognitions are important acknowledgments of the reality of the human condition which his narcissistic impulses had previously banned from his understanding. The most significant and transforming discovery that Achilles makes, however, relates to his new understanding

Understanding the Iliad

of the redemptive power of a richly humane brand of heroism that transcends the expression of that virtue in the limited context provided by war. It is Priam who teaches Achilles this lesson in book 24 through his courageous humility in appearing before him and his willingness, in order to honor Hector, to kiss the hands of the man who has slaughtered so many of his sons. In Priam he sees an image of his own father, old and vulnerable, from whom he is separated and unable to assist because of the war in Troy. Since the death of Patroclus, Achilles has known that suffering is not only what he inflicts on others, but also what he is helpless to deflect from himself. But Priam teaches Achilles by example that suffering can be elevated from the hopeless futility that has devastated him in his tormented, narcissistic state into a meaningful and redemptive experience. Again the insights of Bennett Simon are relevant:[13]

> Thus we see how Homer has elaborated a complex picture of what is needed to resolve the turmoil and sorrow of the human heart. Action alone does not suffice; discharge of emotions is not enough. The acceptance of a common humanity and common mortality begins to achieve some therapeutic effect. At first it only allows Priam and Achilles to mourn at the same time, separately, each for his own sorrows. But the realization that each can empathize with the other brings them closer and allows for something more than pity to surface. Finally, both the disease called "the wrath of Achilles" and the implacable grief of Priam are brought to some resolution *by a profound realization that not only can each be in the other's place but that each has within him parts of all others: man and woman, mother and father, parent and child, sister and brother, friend and foe, beast and human.* (italics mine)

Catharsis as intellectual clarification is at work as forcefully in the *Iliad* as it is in the *Oedipus Rex*. The primary goal of the *Iliad* is not to evoke and purge emotion but to penetrate deeply into the nature and source of powerful, destructive emotions and trace for us the way in which those emotions achieve

Leon Golden

transformation through encounters with bitter experience, as well as with paradigmatic examples of humane heroism. We grasp the totality of the immense achievement of the *Iliad* only when we *understand* how and why the Achilles who was willing to see the entire Achaian army destroyed, who would have been pleased if all the Achaians and Trojans would have perished from the face of the earth, and who, in pursuit of vengeance, brutally massacred his enemies, becomes in the end the Achilles who is capable of conferring mercy and dignity on those who had been the objects of his fierce hatred. Intellectual insight has calmed and transformed the emotions of Achilles and so, too, if emotions are evoked and purged in readers and spectators of the *Iliad* or the *Oedipus Rex*, it is only because the work of art, itself, has guided us to a profound intellectual comprehension of the source, nature, and effect of those emotions.

In the *Iliad,* we do find the experience of oppressive pathos which alienated Plato from the genre of tragedy but we also find the model for the kind of heroic tragedy, the tragedy of *pity and fear*, which Sophocles's *Oedipus Rex* represents and which so strongly influences Aristotle's theory of tragedy in the *Poetics*. And we obtain our most profound appreciation of both the *Iliad* and the *Oedipus Rex, not* through our need for the therapeutic purging of depressing and debilitating emotions, but because of the *emergence of a deepened understanding of complex dimensions of the human condition* that can then, as Bennett Simon reminds us, have a transforming effect on both fictional characters and the living audience alike.

Notes

Introduction

[1] M.M. Willcock, "Some Aspects of the Gods in the *Iliad*," BICS 17 (1970) 3.

[2] M. Edwards, *Homer: the Poet of the Iliad* (Baltimore and London, 1987) 135.

[3] Seth Schein, *The Mortal Hero: An Introduction to Homer's Iliad* (Berkeley and Los Angeles, 1984) 71.

[4] E.T. Owen, *The Story of the Iliad* (Wauconda, IL, 1989) 70-71.

[5] For a discussion of the application of the term "berserk" to Achilles and to a general category of warriors, see Jonathan Shay, *Achilles in Vietnam* (New York, 1995) 77-99.

[6] Walter Burkert, Zum Altgriechischen Mitleidsbegriff (Inaugural-Dissertation der Philosophischen Facultät der Friedrich-Alexander-Universität zu Erlangen, 1955) 114.

[7] *Op. cit.*, 231.

[8] See Harold Cherniss, "The Biographical Fashion in Literary Criticism," *University of California Publications in Classical Philology* 12 (1943) 279-91.

[9] *Homer: His Art and his World:* (Ann Arbor, 1996) 20.

[10] *Op. cit.*, 21.

[11] Seth Schein, *op. cit.*, (Berkeley and Los Angeles, 1984) 1.

Chapter One

[1] M. M. Willcock, *The Iliad of Homer*, Books I-XII, (London, 1978) 196.

[2] *Op. cit.*, 186-87.

[3] *The Iliad of Homer: Books I-XII*, London, 1978) p. 223 (note on line 50).

[4] Jasper Griffin, *Homer on Life and Death* (Oxford, 1980) 197.

[5] G.S. Kirk, *The Iliad: A Commentary*, (Cambridge, 1990) Volume II: books 5-8, 331 note on 11. 427-31 (Greek text).

[6] Cedric Whitman, *Homer and the Heroic Tradition* (Cambridge, Mass., 1958) 241.

[7] See K. Reinhardt, *Tradition und Geist* (Göttingen, 1960) 23-24. He writes: "Bei dem Homerischen Gelächter der Olympier (I, 599), bei dem heiligen unheiligen Schlaf des Zeus in Heras Armen ist nicht zu vergessen, dass Geschichten von List, Fesselung, Aufruhr, Heimlichkeiten der Götter voreinander, die gelegentlich in dunklen Andeutungen auftauchen, auf ein schon vorhomerisches 'Genus' deuten."

[8] *Op. cit.*, 138.

[9] K. Reinhardt, *Die Ilias und ihr Dichter* (Göttingen, 1961) 291 has observed in regard to Hera's actions here that "Was sich im Geheimen abspielt, ist eine Rüstungszene eigner Art. Die Rüstung ist ihre Toilette." For a concise discussion of arming scenes and other type-scenes in Homer, see Edwards, *op. cit.*, 71-77.

[10] U. Hölscher, *Untersuchungen zur Form der Odyssey* (Berlin, 1939) 49.

[11] *Tradition und Geist*, (see note 4) 23-4.

[12] W. Burkert, "Das Lied von Ares und Aphrodite," *Rheinisches Museum* 103 (1960) 140.

[13] B. Seidensticker, *Palintonos Harmonia: Studien zu komischen Elementen in der griechischen Tragodie*, Hypomnemata 72 (Göttingen, 1982) 58.

[14] *Op. cit.*, 195.

[15] *Op. cit.*, 189-90.

[16] *Op. cit.*, 190.

[17] *Op. cit.*, 181-83.

[18] *Op. cit.*, 71.

[19] *Op. cit.*, 70-71.

[20] See his chapter in *Mortals and Immortals* ed. by F. Zeitlin (Princeton, 1991) 50-74. The chapter was originally published in its original French version as an essay entitled "La belle mort et le cadavre outragé" published in G. Gnioli and J.-P. Vernant, *La mort, les morts dans les sociétés anciennes* (Cambridge and Paris, 1982) 45-76.

[21] Bernard Knox, "Premature Anti-Fascist," *The First Annual Abraham Lincoln Brigade Archives-Bill Sussman* Lecture (New York, 1998) 9.

[22] R. Renehan, "The *Heldentod* in Homer: One Heroic Ideal," *Classical Philology* 82 (1987) 99-116.

[23] *Op. cit.*, 110-11.

[24] *Op. cit.*, 31.

[25] *Op. cit.*, 58-59.

[26] M. Willcock, *The Iliad of Homer*, Books I-XII (London, 1978) 262-63.

[27] G.S. Kirk, *The Iliad: A Commentary*, vol. II, books 5-8, 306.

[28] *Op. cit.*, Ch. IV, 103-43.

Chapter Two

1. For a detailed discussion of how Homer accomplishes this, see Latacz, *op. cit.,* 71-133.
2. *Op. cit.,* 133.
3. See *Poetics,* 1450 b26-31 where Aristotle defines the terms, "beginning, [middle], and end" so that the beginning requires nothing by necessity or probability to occur before it, the end requires something by necessity and probability to occur before it but nothing after it, and the middle requires something by necessity or probability to occur both before it and after it.
4. Latacz, *op. cit.,* 77.
5. M.M. Willcock, *The Iliad of Homer,* Books I-XII (London, 1978) 185.
6. See Mark Edwards, *op. cit.,* 179.
7. See Kirk, *op. cit.,* 61-62 (general comments on lines 85-91 and specific comments on lines 90-91.)
8. *Op. cit.,* 96.
9. See Jonathan Shay, *Achilles in Vietnam* (New York, 1995) 125-27 for a discussion of fragging. Shay describes the encounter between Agamemnon and Achilles as an "interrupted fragging."
10. J. Griffin ed., *Homer: Iliad IX* (Oxford, 1995) 109-10.
11. Griffin, *op. cit.,* (note 10), 21.
12. *Op. cit.,* 97.
13. *Op. cit.,* 231-32.
14. *Op. cit.,* 231.
15. *Op. cit.,* 232.
16. *Op. cit.,* 235.
17. *Op. cit.,* 233, 234, 235.
18. Bryan Hainsworth, *The Iliad: A Commentary* (Cambridge, 1993) vol. III: books 9-12, note on 11. 643-55, pp. 143-44.
19. A. Lowen, *Narcissism: Denial of the True Self* (New York, 1985) 92-94.
20. B. Hainsworth, *op. cit.,* vol. III: books 9-12, 289 (note on 11. 608-15).
21. *Op. cit.,* 98-99.
22. James Masterson, *The Narcissistic and Borderline Disorders* (New York, 1981) 182, 185.
23. Thomas J. Brady, "Making Peace: Youth and Drugs and Violence," *San Francisco Medical Society* (July 1998) 71 (6); "Incident at SFO—Considering Violence in Adolescent Males," *San Francisco Medical Society* (October 2001) 74 (1).
24. O. Taplin, "The Shield of Achilles Within the *Iliad,*" *Greece & Rome* 27 (1980) 1-21.
25. *Op. cit.,* 12.
26. *Op. cit.,* 188.

27 *Op. cit.,* 194.
28 S. Schein, *The Mortal Hero* (Berkeley and Los Angeles, 1984) 145.
29 *Op. cit.,* 229.
30 Quoted by Owen, *op. cit.,* 232.
31 *Op. cit.,* 235.
32 *Op. cit.,* 156.
33 *Op. cit.,* 162.
34 *Op. cit.,* 90.
35 N. Richardson, *The Iliad: A Commentary,* vol. VI: books 21-24, 189 (note on line 176).
36 *Op. cit.,* 75.
37 *Op. cit.,* 227 (note on 11.532-3).
38 *Op. cit.,* 236 (note on line 621).
39 *Op. cit.,* 100.
40 *Zum Altgrichischen Mitleidsbegriff* (Inaugural-Dissertation der Philosophischen Facultät zu Erlangen (1955) 104-06, 114.
41 *Op. cit.,* 337 (note on 11.582-90).
42 G. Zanker, *The Heart of Achilles* (Ann Arbor, 1994) 149.
43 C.W. Macleod, *Homer: Iliad, Book XXIV* (Cambridge, 1982) 8.

Chapter Three

1 See *Republic* 605-607.
2 E.R. Dodds, *Euripides: Bacchae* (Oxford, 1960) xx, xliii.
3 *Op. cit.,* xlv.
4 *Op. cit.,* 196-97.
5 *Poetics,* 1453a1-17. Translations of passages from the *Poetics* here and below are reprinted with permission of the University Press of Florida from L. Golden and O.B. Hardison, Jr., *Aristotle's Poetics: A Translation and Commentary for Students of Literature* (University Press of Florida (Gainesville, FL, 1981).
6 E.R. Dodds, "On Misunderstanding the *Oedipus Rex,*" *Greece and Rome* 13 (1966) 37-49. The passages cited are from pages 39 and 43.
7 *Politics,* 1341b36-1342a16.
8 G.F. Else, *Aristotle's Poetics: The Argument* (Cambridge, Mass., 1957) 440.
9 *Poetics,* 1448b4- 17. For a detailed discussion of Aristotle's theory of tragedy and catharsis see L. Golden, *Aristotle on Tragic and Comic Mimesis* (Atlanta, 1992).
10 *Poetics* 1450b21-1341a15.
11 *Poetics* 1451a33-34.
12 Bennett Simon, *Mind and Madness in Ancient Greece: the Classical Roots of Modern Psychiatry* (Ithaca and London, 1978) 144-45.
13 *Op. cit.,* 76.

Index

A

Aristotle viii, 38, 64, 126, 135, 136, 137, 139, 140, 141, 143, 144, 145, 146, 147, 150, 153, 154

B

Bildungsroman xviii, xxii, 39, 82, 102
Brady, Thomas J. 85, 116, 153
Burkert, Walter xvii, 9, 119, 151, 152

C

Cherniss, Harold xviii, xix, xx, xxi, 151

D

Dodds, E.R. 128, 129, 132, 133, 139, 140, 154
Double motivation xiii, xiv, 19, 44, 73, 84, 116

E

Edwards, Mark xiii, xviii, 3, 64, 65, 66, 67, 69, 71, 151, 152, 153
Else, G.F. 143, 145, 154

G

Golden, Leon viii, 154
Griffin, Jasper 4, 10, 11, 12, 33, 63, 64, 151, 153

H

Hainsworth, Bryan 71, 75, 77, 153
Heroic code ix, xii, xiv, xv, xvi, xvii, xxii, 13, 14, 15, 16, 19, 20, 21, 22, 23, 24, 25, 26, 27, 28, 29, 30, 31, 32, 33, 34, 35, 36, 37, 43, 48, 53, 54, 59, 61, 86, 100, 119, 125, 131
Hölscher, U. 9, 152

K

Kirk, G.S. 4, 27, 152, 153
Knox, Bernard 18, 20, 152

L

Latacz, Joachim xxi, xxii, 38, 39, 42, 153
Lex talionis 60, 67, 84, 85, 92, 102, 114, 116, 124
Lowen, Alexander 72, 73, 74, 75, 78, 81, 82, 107, 108, 109, 110, 114, 118, 153

M

MacLeod, C.W. 123
Masterson, James 85, 153

N

Narcissism 82, 83, 109, 110, 113, 137, 142, 148, 153

O

Owen, E.T. xv, 5, 6, 14, 15, 23, 24, 64, 89, 90, 101, 102, 106, 151, 154

P

Pathos vii, xii, xiv, xvii, xviii, xxii, 21, 29, 33, 34, 35, 63, 110, 127, 131, 133, 135, 136, 137, 148, 150

Plato 126, 135, 136, 137, 145, 150

Poetics viii, 126, 136, 137, 143, 144, 145, 150, 153, 154

Politics 143, 154

R

Reinhardt, Karl 5, 9, 86, 152

Renehan, Robert 19, 20, 21, 152

Richardson, N. 108, 111, 113, 121, 154

S

Schein, Seth xiv, xv, 13, 19, 96, 102, 103, 151, 154

Seidensticker, Bernd 9, 72, 152

Shay, Jonathan 151, 153

Simon, Bennett 146, 149, 150, 154

T

Taplin, Oliver 86, 87, 88, 89, 91, 92, 93, 94, 153

Tragedy vii, xiv, 9, 18, 64, 101, 115, 126, 127, 128, 131, 133, 135, 136, 137, 138, 139, 140, 143, 144, 145, 146, 147, 148, 150, 154

V

Vernant, J-P. xv, xvi, 16, 17, 18, 19, 25, 152

W

Whitman, Cedric 5, 152

Wilamowitz-Moellendorff, Ulrich von xviii, xix, xx, xxi

Willcock, M.M. x, xii, 2, 3, 27, 151, 152, 153

Z

Zanker, Graham 123, 154

About The Author

Throughout his academic career, Professor Golden has focused his teaching and research interests on Greek tragedy, Homer, and classical literary criticism, and has published a number of articles and books in these areas. One of his principal interests has been in demonstrating that Aristotle's famous doctrine of catharsis—traditionally understood as a form of purgation of troubling emotions—should actually be understood as the process of intellectual clarification of the cause, nature, and effect of those emotions. In his analysis of the Iliad, he applies this doctrine of catharsis to Homer's great epic poem. Until his recent retirement, Professor Golden was professor of classics and director of the Program in Humanities at Florida State University.

CPSIA information can be obtained at www.ICGtesting.com
234319LV00001B/169/A